MOB TIES 3

SAYNOMORE

Lock Down Publications and Ca$h
Presents

MOB TIES 3

A Novel by *SAYNOMORE*

SAYNOMORE

Lock Down Publications
P.O. Box 944
Stockbridge, Ga 30281
www.lockdownpublications.com

Copyright 2021 by SAYNOMORE
Mob Ties 3

Lock Down Publications
Like our page on Facebook: Lock Down Publications @
www.facebook.com/lockdownpublications.ldp

Book interior design by: **Shawn Walker**
Edited by: **Shamika Smith**

Acknowledgements

First, I would like to thank my Lord and savior, Jesus Christ, for all the blessings in my life and all the hard times for walking me through them. I want to thank all of my children: Chammorro, Jataya, Jelani and Sharese Jr for loving me unconditionally because y'all push me to be a better father. I want to thank my mother, Rafanella, and my auntie mom, Evada, for everything they done for me in my life. Also, my Auntie Nan for loving me unconditionally. And a big shout out to Deyasmin Parkinson. I want to thank all of my loyal readers for their support for following MOB TIES. Much love goes to all of y'all. Respect and Love.

Stay Connected with Us!

Text **LOCKDOWN** to 22828 to stay up-to-date with new releases, sneak peaks, contests and more...

Thank you!

Submission Guideline.

Submit the first three chapters of your completed manuscript to ldpsubmissions@gmail.com, subject line: Your book's title. The manuscript must be in a .doc file and sent as an attachment. Document should be in Times New Roman, double spaced and in size 12 font. Also, provide your synopsis and full contact information. If sending multiple submissions, they must each be in a separate email.

Have a story but no way to send it electronically? You can still submit to LDP/Ca$h Presents. Send in the first three chapters, written or typed, of your completed manuscript to:

LDP: Submissions Dept
P.O. Box 944
Stockbridge, Ga 30281

DO NOT send original manuscript. Must be a duplicate.

Provide your synopsis and a cover letter containing your full contact information.

Thanks for considering LDP and Ca$h Presents.

SAYNOMORE

Chapter 1

Jatavious was watching *60 Minutes* live as they had a live interview with Chief Tafem of the 33 NYC police present. The police chief and the TV show host were discussing the underground crime ring.

"So, Chief Anthony Red, what is the city of NY doing about this crime wave sweeping NYC and leaving a body count everywhere they go?"

"That's a good question and as of right now, New York City police are working with a special criminal unit to slow down this bloody crime wave in NYC. We have agents working day and night on several cases, Mrs. Smith."

"Chief Tafem, are the rumors true that there is a black female don running this crime ring?"

"No, there are no truths to the rumors that we know of as of right now."

"What steps are you taking to find the leak in the police department to find the mole who leaked out Mr. Deniro's whereabouts that got him killed five months ago on a prison transporting bus?"

"At the moment we do believe that the reason that DA Moore was assassinated was that he was crooked. And whoever assassinated him didn't want it to get out who he was working with; that is, if he was working with anybody in the underground criminal world. It's still in the air if he did give Mr. Deniro's whereabouts up. It was only a few people who knew about the transporting of Mr. Deniro. The guards who were transporting him found out who they were transporting at the time and day they were to transport Mr. Deniro."

"Are you saying that DA Moore was getting paid under the table by the mafia?"

"I'm saying we are looking into all possibilities as of right now until this case is solved. I have a list of public figures who were killed over the years, starting with Mayor Oakland all the way down to DA Moore, including big wigs of the mafia. A name that is known very well is Tony Lenacci, the boss of all bosses, better known as "the Untouchable Don". Again, Mrs. Smith, we are working day and night, pulling all strings to end this bloody crime wave."

Jatavious cut the TV off after watching half of Chief Tafem's interview with *60 Minutes*. He always knew that Red Invee was a silent killer, and that she would change the underground criminal world to fit around her. Earlier that year when she had Deniro killed, Jatavious knew then she was becoming too powerful. Just hearing the interview with Chief Tafem, he knew she got to him. Somehow, he knew that Red Invee had an angel looking over her even though she was the devil's child.

He walked to his bar, and poured a shot of gin to honor Red Invee. After all, he did respect her even though he knew she had to die, and the clock was ticking.

Chapter 2

Frankie sat outside his house, smoking his cigar and drinking shots of brandy, thinking about how he and Jamila haven't talked in a while. He loved her as if she were his daughter. He was thinking back about how their cars were shot up multiple times after they were set up by Mr. Deniro. As he was lying on the floor of his car, he was hoping Red Invee was okay and to see her get out of her car put a smile on his face. Months passed, and Frankie and Jamila haven't talked and he knew it was time to clear up the air. So, he made an appointment to have lunch with her and Lorenzo tomorrow afternoon at Destiny's. Not knowing how things might turn out, he knew it was about time they got back to where they once were.

***

"Jamila, you alright?"

"Yea, I'm just waiting to get this day over with."

"So, what you think Frankie want?"

"I don't know, Lorenzo, but after all, I do owe it to him to hear what he got to say."

"Jamila, you don't owe that man nothing. Look at all you did for him."

"Lorenzo, I could buy him the world, but what he did for us I could never replace."

"But you got back all of his kilos of cocaine, ran his family for him, got him a new house, do I need to go on? What more do you owe him?"

"Lorenzo, he gave us our lives back. If it wasn't for him we would be dead. He helped us build this family we have now. He was there for us when no one else was. I understand he turned his back against us, but you know what, Lorenzo? I will never forget the hand that fed me, but I won't be a sucker for it. Now come on, I don't want to be late."

When they arrived, Frankie was sitting down, talking to Fabio at the bar. Fabio had on an all-white suit with a red dress shirt, a white tie and red shoes with no socks. His hair was curly, and he was rocking a goatee with a fresh tapeline and a diamond-encrusted Rolex watch on with a small T-bone gold chain. Frankie had on a black suit with a Kangol hat, a white shirt with no tie, and an all-black pair of Stacy Adams while smoking a cigar when Lorenzo and Jamila walked in.

Jamila had on a red dress that hugged her body, with a black mink coat and some black open-toed shoes. Her hair was in kinky twists coming down her face, which was accentuated by a pair of Louis Vuitton sunglasses. Lorenzo had on some blue jeans and a white dress shirt, with a pair of white sneakers and a New York Mets baseball cap.

Frankie got up, hugged Jamila, and shook Lorenzo's hand. Fabio did the same thing as Frankie, but he kissed Jamila on both cheeks.

"Frankie, can you tell me why we are here?"

"Jamila, as always, it's a pleasure to see you and I know we haven't talked in a while, but that's on my end, not yours, and because of my wrongdoing. I want to put everything on the table. So, what I'm asking is for everything that needs to be said, let's say it. We are all too close and came too far to fall out like this over lies and misunderstandings."

Jamila nodded. "You're right, Frankie, so who wants to talk first?"

"I will," said Frankie. Getting up, Frankie looked at Jamila and said, "Six years ago I told Fabio to fake his death to disappear for a little while because I didn't want to see him get killed. He told me no a few times, but I told him I will take care of you and to just go. At the time, I thought that was the best thing for him. Jamila, I knew nothing of you, nor did I know if I could trust you, but in the end I was wrong. I did what I thought was best. After a few months, I was going to tell you Fabio was alive, but I didn't because I didn't want to bring up an old flame while you were at war, so I apologize about that. You are like a daughter to me, so I shouldn't have lied or done anything to you. That was wrong, and I know I broke the ground of loyalty we once stood on."

Jamila knew Frankie was telling the truth.

"Jamila, I ain't say nothing, but the day I left the pond I over-heard you talking to Deniro over the phone, what was I supposed to think? The man who tried to kill me shot up my house and put a bomb in one of Fabio's cars. I hear you talking to him, so what would you think?"

She knew what he was saying was right, so she didn't say a word.

"There's nothing I can say to you, Jamila, to show how truly sorry I am."

"Jamila, what Frankie is saying is true," said Fabio, as he got up and walked to her. "I have never stopped loving you. I know I hurt you in more ways than one and no woman should ever endure. But, not one day went by that I wasn't thinking about you. It hurt me so bad not being with you, Jamila."

Jamila really loved Fabio with all of her heart, and he was her strength. She closed her eyes, and lowered her head as tears started to fall down her face. She hated Fabio and Frankie so much, but she also loved them. As she got up, she looked around the bar at them and said, "Frankie, you lied to me for years and Fabio you left me for years, so I don't have the right to be upset? I got shot over you, Fabio, and I killed two of my friends over you because they tried to set you up, and one was not loyal to what we stand on. I can be real and tell you I was scared and you weren't there for me. I woke up in the middle of the night sometimes calling your name, and where were you in Paris?"

"Jamila, I'm so sorry, I am," as he walked up to her.

He grabbed her hand and pulled her to him and she laid her head on his shoulders. As she was crying, he picked her head up looking into her eyes, and kissed her tears.

"Jamila, as I stand here, I want to say I truly love you with a deep love that no one can ever imagine. So, I'm asking you here and now, will you be my wife?"

Without saying a word, she nodded. "Yes, I will, Fabio, I will marry you."

Fabio picked her up and kissed her like never before.

Chapter 3

"Yo, Badii, what's good, homie? I haven't seen you in a minute, homie."

"What the fuck is rocking, Masi? What's really good?"

"Just trying to eat, you know how I move already, big facts. I know you're trained to go."

"I heard you with the LaCross family now and you're one of the top Lt's."

"Yo, Masi, I don't know shit about no murder, but here is my number. We need to link up."

"Bet that up, Badii. When you want me to play your line?"

"Hit me this weekend."

"Peace, dog."

"Alright, my nigga."

As Badii got in his 2003 BMW, he passed Youngboy the bag that was in his hand.

"Who was that, Badii?"

"A real hitta hands down. That's my round—Masi. I'm plugging him in with Red Invee. He's a one-time ask type of nigga and it's done. We need homies like that in the family."

"Yo, why Lorenzo got us meeting him at Red Hook Projects?" asked Youngboy.

"The fuck if I know. He just told me to pull up with you and make sure we holding, that's all," replied Badii.

"I stay with my bitch and she quick to bust a nut."

"I already know, Youngboy."

As Badii pulled up in Red Hook Projects, he saw Lorenzo leaning against his car.

"Yo, Lorenzo, what's good?"

"Shit, just a little problem we need to take care of really quick with this nigga named Ace and his little crew."

"Fuck it, let's get this shit over with," said Youngboy.

Lorenzo walked up on Ace and his crew while they were rolling dice. He kicked the dice while they were still rolling. Ace looked up at him.

"I don't give a fuck about what you are thinking, but let it get you fucked up, little nigga."

Ace looked at Badii and Youngboy, and he knew Youngboy for killing shit. He lowered his hand to tell his boys to cool down. Lorenzo looked at him when he did it.

"I'm glad we got an understanding now. I got a message for you, Ace. Red Invee said go play somewhere else because there is already a dog in this backyard, and this is the only time she's going to tell you this. Next time you will be cleaning up blood."

Ace looked at him as he patted Badii on the chest and walked off.

"Yo, Ace, who the fuck that boy thinks he is?"

"A dead man, dog. Fuck him, come on let's roll out. I know what I'm going to do. Fuck Red Invee, my heart doesn't pump Kool-Aid for her, that bitch can die too and we still ain't going no fucking where. We going to see who will be cleaning up blood."

Chapter 4

"So, how it go with Ace?"

"I told him word for word what you said, Jamila."

"Good, I hope he gets the picture; if not, fuck him and black-bag his ass. I'm about to go see Frankie, Lorenzo."

"Give him my love."

"I will," said Jamila, as she walked out of her office.

It's been a few weeks since Fabio asked Jamila to marry him. She pulled up at Frankie's house, and got out. After his guards let him know she was there, they walked her to him in the backyard next to the pool. Frankie was smoking a cigar. When he saw Jamila, he got up, hugged her and gave her a kiss on the cheek.

"So tell me, Jamila, what brings you by?"

"To tell you the truth, I have never been here before. Lorenzo got the house and I just paid for it."

"Well, thank you! There's something I always wanted to ask."

"And what's that, Frankie?"

"I always wanted to ask you about your childhood. Tell me your story because I want to know why you move the way you do and why you think how you think."

"Frankie, I really don't like talking about my childhood, but for you, I will. From the time I was eight years old, my father always talked about loyalty to me, so he got me a puppy. My father told me to treat her like my best friend, and one that will always be loyal to me. My father had a way with words. He never showed his emotions at all. My father was a businessman, and my mother was a school teacher. So, anyway, he told me loyalty will take you a long way. A few minutes later, there was a knock at the door, and it was my father's friend who came to see him. They talked for a few minutes, then he left. After that, my father came inside, picked me up and said: 'I love you, sweet pea!'

A few days passed, and it was around 10 p.m. that night when we heard a sound at the door. The door flew off the hinges, and three guys ran in, and they beat my father really bad. I was under my bed, and my father's room was right across from mine. When my door opened, I saw and heard footsteps and then I saw them go back out the room. My father was on the floor, bleeding badly, and all I saw was a man hitting him over and over again. For one second, I and my father made eye contact before they picked him up and made him watch how they beat and raped my mother over and over again. They must have thought they killed him. As for my mother, they told her if she tells they would do the same thing to me. If she told, they would find out.

As I laid on the floor, I heard them as they left. My mother untied my dad, but at that time he was unconscious, but he came around a few minutes later. I ran to him and hugged him. My mother was in a lot of pain. That night my father made us leave after he burned the house down. A few days went by, and my father got a phone call, and he told the man that it was his turn now. He gave me two books, *The 48 Laws of Power* and *The Art of War*. He said life is a circle and the past will always come back; but if you read about what's happening to others, you won't have to worry about it happening to you. That night, my father and his best friend went to visit his business partner, but what my father did not know was that his best friend was an unloyal rat that set him up. The gun he gave my father had no bullets in it at all. See, I was too young to know this story my mother told me. She told me it was his best friend that set him up. They sent a video tape to my mother of them cutting my father into pieces alive. Fingers, hands, and cutting his muscles right off the bone while he was still alive and tied up. After ten minutes, you saw someone with a gun put it to the back of his head and pull the trigger, killing him. My mother never showed me this tape but I found it and I cried and cried, looking at him getting tortured and cut into pieces. So, I promised myself that when I found out who did this, they would pay with their life. So, the last thing my father said was to read the books. I studied them for years. His killers were never found, and all I did was study what he told me to do."

"Jamila, what is your father's name?" asked Frankie.

"Anthony Catwell."

"I knew it. I had a feeling you was going to say that name."

"You know him?" asked Jamila.

"Yes, I did, I knew him very well. He was the best when it came down to dealing with problems that had to be dealt with. And with numbers, he would tell you every penny of your money."

"Frankie, tell me something about my father I didn't know."

"Jamila, your father and Tony were very close friends. When Tony needed a problem taken care of, he would call your father. I don't remember the whole story clearly, but I do remember bits and pieces of it. Tony had a big drug deal taking place, and your father was there. It was about ten to fifteen million, but I'm not sure. Felipe Carlione was trying to get over on Tony, and your father pointed out how much money Tony would be losing out on. Felipe was pissed off, and two days later he sent Jatavious Stone to go talk to your father."

"Wait, Jatavious Stone set my father up?" Jamila asked.

"Yes and when your father told him he would not work with him, he left. Your father was loyal to Tony. I just told Fabio this same story, but I ain't let him know it was Jatavious or Felipe who was with Timmy Guns. Jamila, I killed Timmy Guns."

"So why ain't you kill Jatavious or Felipe?"

"At the time of your father's death, Jatavious and Felipe were too strong. Me and Tony ain't have the manpower to take them on. When they sent the video, Felipe also sent a note that said even the boogeyman got killed at the end of the movie. But what Tony did was, give your mother one hundred thousand dollars every year for you for seven years. He knew it couldn't bring your father back, but he tried to help heal the pain as much as he could."

Jamila sat there with tears in her eyes, as Frankie told her the story of her father's death.

"All this time I was taking pictures with Jatavious and smiling in his face, and he killed my father."

"He might not even know who you are. I'm sure he is just as in the blind as I was to who your father was."

"Frankie, how can I find this Felipe?" she asked while wiping tears from her eyes.

"This is not no city mob, Felipe is the real deal."

"I want to meet him, Frankie, can you set it up for me?"

"I'll see what I can do. He has people under him, and he really doesn't meet new people."

"But I'm with you, Frankie, and that's my door to see him."

"Okay, I'll see what I can do. Now he is about his business, so what are you going to bring to the table?"

"Three million dollars," said Jamila.

"I'll make the call."

"Thank you, Frankie."

"Don't thank me just yet. Let me see what I can do first. So give me a few days to try and put something together."

Jamila got up and kissed Frankie on the forehead before walking off.

Chapter 5

Badii was leaning against his car parked outside of Eazy Deal, drinking a soda when he saw Masi walking up. He had on a black hoodie, black sweatpants, and black timbs, with his right hand in his pocket.

"Yo, Badii, what's good, my guy?"

"Shit, waiting on you to pull up. Get in, let's take a ride. Yo, Masi, you sure this is the move you want to make because Red Invee stands on loyalty, and her number one rule is: the first time you fuck up—you die."

Masi looked at Badii and said, "I'm ready, bruh."

"That's what I wanted to hear. Look around, bruh, Red Invee runs all of this, but you will never see her. That's what she got us for. We are the killers in the streets, but don't get it fucked up. She done killed just as many motherfuckers as we have in the most bloodiest way you can think of."

"So where we headed now?" asked Masi.

Badii looked at him with a smile on his face, and said: "We're going to meet the queen!"

Looking out the window, Masi just nodded. He'd heard stories about Red Invee, and now—for the first time—he was going to meet her face to face. When Badii pulled up in front of *Jelani's Restaurant*, Masi saw two men outside dressed in suits real clean. Then he cut his eye at Badii, noticing he was also dressed tight and not like a thug.

"Come on, let's get inside, Masi."

As they walked inside, one of the guys stopped Masi at the door and patted him down, then took his gun off him and placed it in a black box. He looked at Badii.

"She doesn't know you, and rules are rules, Masi. This ain't the block, this is the mob. Come on, let's go see the Don."

When they walked into Red Invee's office, she was sitting outside on the deck, eating her breakfast, talking to Lorenzo. When they walked out to the deck, Masi looked at her. He had never seen such a beautiful female like her before.

"Badii, this must be Masi you was telling me about."

"Yes, Jamila."

"Masi, this is Jamila and Lorenzo."

"Nice to finally meet you, Jamila and Lorenzo."

"Nice to meet you too," said Lorenzo, as he went to shake his hand.

"Masi, have a seat. So, Badii told me a little bit about you, and now that I have you here tell me, Masi, would I ever have to second guess you?"

"No, Mrs. LaCross, I stand on loyalty."

"I hope you do because Badii put his face on your name. If you're going to be a part of this family, I'm going to have to be able to trust you at all times, Masi," stated Jamila.

"I'm never going to give you a reason not to trust me, Mrs. LaCross."

"Good. My three rules are: respect the code of silence; the first time you fuck up, you die; and when I tell *you* to take care of somebody, *you* bring me back the head as proof. I don't want Lorenzo, Badii, not even Youngboy to do it. I want *you* to do it when I tell you to. Do you understand that?"

"Yes, I do."

"Good because everyone gets their hands bloody in my family. Word got back to me that Ace and his crew think I'm a game, and they're still in Red Hook Projects. So Masi, Ace's right-hand man's name is Dog, I believe?"

"Yes, it is, Jamila," Lorenzo stated, as she was looking at him.

"Okay, Masi, just go get Dog and no one else, and bring me back my proof."

When Masi got up and was about to walk out, Jamila stopped him.

"Masi," she called.

"Yes."

"You have seventy-two hours from now," replied Jamila.

Walking out the door with Badii, Masi didn't say a word until they got back in the car.

"What the fuck, bruh? Is she dead ass?"

Badii nodded. "Yeah, she is. Welcome to the mob. What she ain't tell you is if you don't take care of it within that time, one of us will. Then she will have you killed."

Masi shook his head and gave Badii a pound before getting out of the car in front of Red Hook.

"Yo, Masi," said Badii, "before you get out just know she was dead ass serious about that head proof."

Masi nodded as he got out and closed the door.

SAYNOMORE

Chapter 6

"Lorenzo, in a few days I'm leaving with Frankie to Mexico to see the man who killed my father."

"Wait, Jamila, Frankie knows the man who killed your father?" replied Lorenzo.

"Yeah, he does, and guess who else had a part in his death with blood on their hands?"

"Who?"

"Jatavious Stone, but none of them knew it was my father nor do they know I'm his child."

"So, you think it's smart to go down there?" asked Lorenzo.

"I need to look in his eyes, Lorenzo. I can't say I stand on loyalty and know the man who killed my father is still walking around and I ain't do nothing."

"So, what you going to say to him?" asked Lorenzo.

"I don't know. Hold on, my phone is going off. Hello?"

"Hey, Jamila. I talked to Felipe and he's agreed to meet us in three days, so make sure you are at my house Tuesday morning by three a.m. We are going to have a private plane waiting for us."

"Okay, I'll be ready, and thank you again, Frankie. That was Frankie, he told me we leave in three days. While I'm gone, make sure Masi takes care of Dog and if he doesn't kill him—No, better yet have Badii kill him since he brought him to my table. Now I have to go and see Fabio and I'll catch up with you later."

***

"Hey beautiful, how is my wife-to-be doing today?"

"I'm doing good. I miss you so much, bae."

"You do?" exclaimed Fabio with a smile on his face. "So how about I take you out to lunch?"

"I'm so ready, that sounds good to me. So, where will you be taking me?" asked Jamila.

"Now that's a surprise!"

"Don't do that, baby, where are you taking me to lunch at?"

"Do you really want to know?"

"Yes, I do."

"Okay, we're going on my yacht to have lunch."

Jamila smiled and hugged him. After eating, she just looked at the sea.

"Fabio, I love it out here, I do, it's so beautiful and peaceful!"

Fabio wrapped his hands around her, and kissed her on the neck.

"Fabio baby, we need to talk."

"Come on, bae, let's go talk down in the den of the yacht."

Fabio sat on the love seat, and Jamila laid across the couch and laid her head on his lap.

"So, what is it you wanted to talk to me about, baby?" asked Fabio.

"I found out who was the man who killed my father, and Frankie is going to take me to see him this week."

"Jamila, are you sure you are ready to see this man?"

"Yes and no, but the video of my father being killed just keeps playing in my mind over and over. The nightmares I've been having for the last twenty-three years got to come to an end."

"Jamila, I know how you felt about your father and I know how much you loved him. I do, but you have a whole mafia family here that needs you. Whatever you want to do, I'm with you, but just know it's not going to bring him back. Tell me, who is the man who killed your father?"

She rolled over and looked up at him.

"Felipe has my father's blood on his hands.

"Mexican drug lord Felipe Carlione? And Frankie is taking you to his house?" said Fabio.

"Yes, he is, and I'm not worried about how powerful he is or was."

"I know you're not, baby, but he is a cold-blooded killer and he bleeds just like me and you, bae."

"I'm just going to meet him, that's all," replied Jamila.

"I just want you to think nigger when it comes to Felipe. I'm sure he already knows who you are. Just know whatever you want to do, just know I'm with you till my last breath."

Jamila listened to every word Fabio said, and didn't say a word. Everything he was saying was right.

"Baby, listen, I just want you to think about what I'm saying, that's it."

"I am, baby, I am."

Fabio hugged Jamila, and kissed her on the forehead.

"I love you, Jamila!"

"I love you more, Fabio!"

SAYNOMORE

Chapter 7

Jamila got out of the car Tuesday morning at Frankie's house. She looked around because it was dark and cold outside. Frankie opened up the front door to let her in.

"Are you ready for today?" asked Frankie.

"Yeah, I am."

"Good, the car is on the way now."

"Why do we have a car coming to pick us up?"

"Because of the level he is on; it's his rules or nothing. Felipe is a very powerful man. What do you have in the bag?"

Jamila showed him her pink 9mm and $100k in cash. Frank looked out the window, and saw headlights coming down the driveway.

"Come in, that's our ride."

Within forty-five minutes they were aboard Felipe's private plane. Jamila looked at Frankie, and he nodded to her to let her know everything was going to be okay. Four hours on the plane, and it landed. This was the second time Jamila was meeting a Mexican drug lord. The car was ready to take them to Felipe Carlione's cartel house. When the car pulled up, Felipe was outside. He couldn't wait to meet Jamila because he'd heard so many stories about her. Jamila looked around, and she was shocked because Felipe was very comfortable. He was so used to having his way. He wasn't worried about anybody. The car stopped, and Felipe walked up to the car as they stepped out.

"Frankie, it's good to see you, old friend," Felipe said, as he shook his hand.

"It's good to see you too, how you been?"

"I've been good, and this beautiful female must be Jamila." Felipe walked up to her, and kissed her on both cheeks.

"How are you, Jamila?"

"I'm good, Felipe, thank you for seeing me."

"No, thank you for coming. I've heard so many stories about you. Now I have the chance of meeting you."

"Please don't listen to those stories."

"So Jamila, what can I do for you?"

"Mr. Felipe, can we go somewhere and talk?"

"Yes, follow me."

Felipe walked them to the patio of his $23M mansion.

"Please have a seat so we can talk. So tell me, Jamila, what can I do for you?"

The more she looked at him, the more she wanted to kill him. She kept on seeing the man who killed her father in a gruesome way.

"Felipe, I would like to do some business with you."

"Sure, what kind of business?"

"Well, Frankie told me you are the perfect one to shop with on pure powder."

Felipe looked at Frankie, then back at Jamila.

"He was right, I am."

"So what deals will you give me?"

"That depends on how much money you are going to spend with me," said Felipe.

"Three million five hundred thousand dollars"

"I'll give you each kilo of cocaine for seven thousand dollars. So, we're talking numbers around five hundred thousand kilos. And how you plan on moving them back up to NY?"

"That's what I need you for, Felipe," said Jamila.

"So, how would you be paying me?"

"Bank to bank, is that alright with you?"

"That works fine. Frankie, I like this one."

For the next two hours Frankie, Felipe, and Jamila laughed and joked. When it was time to leave, Felipe gave Jamila his number, and told her the drop will be in seventy-two hours. Frankie and Jamila didn't talk on the way home. When they were back at Frankie's house, he looked at her.

"Jamila, how are you going to move that much weight? Not to mention you already have so much coming from Morwell."

"I don't know, Frankie, but let me think about it. Thank you for everything."

Chapter 8

Masi looked at his watch and saw it was 7 p.m. Today was the last day for him to take care of that business. He'd been watching Dog for two days now, making plays and running from spot to spot in Red Hook. He ain't seen Ace at all in them two days, but he knew Dog has been at Tonya's spot. He watched as Dog was walking through the playground, smoking a blunt.

"Dog, pull up for a second."

"Yo, who the fuck is that?" said Dog.

"Masi, my nigga."

"Yo, what's rocking? I ain't seen you in a minute. Where the fuck you been?"

"Trapping it out," replied Masi.

"Facts, I feel you on that. That's how I'm eating over here all the way caked up."

"Word, you got that work?"

"What you looking for, Masi?"

"Two ounces if you got them."

"Shit, that's going to run you one thousand four hundred dollars apiece."

"Facts, I got that now."

"Shit! Come with me, let's take care of that business then."

"I'm waiting on you."

Walking into Tonya's apartment, Masi saw her coming from the back room.

"Yo, Masi, post up and I'll go get that for you, homie." When Dog came back, Masi handed him $2800.

"That's what the fuck I'm talking about. Here you go, that's that good shit eighty-five percent pure."

In the twinkling of an eye, Masi pulled out on Dog.

"Yo, what the fuck you got going on!" yelled Dog.

"Red Invee said she told you to stop playing with her."

"Man, fuck that bitch! She can suck my dick, nigga."

"Big facts. Fuck her, right? No! Fuck you, nigga and suck on this."

Masi shot Dog three times in the face, and Tonya started to scream.

"Shut the fuck up, bitch," said Masi.

"Please don't kill me, please don't."

"Bitch, please," he said, as he pointed the gun at her and shot her three times in the chest.

"*Please don't kill me,*" Masi said, mimicking Tonya, as he gazed at her dead body. "Bitch, you sound dumb as fuck." Masi put his gun up, and grabbed a knife from the kitchen. He got down on one knee, and started to cut Dog's head off.

Chapter 9

Jamila walked into Jelani's to her office, picked up her phone, and called Lorenzo.

"Hey, what's up, Jamila?"

"Where you at?"

"I'm on my way to Jelani's now."

"Good because we need to talk. I'm in my office waiting on you," said Jamila.

"I'll be there in twenty minutes tops."

After hanging up the phone, Jamila walked to her desk and sat down, turning on the TV. She caught the last ten minutes of the news. The story was being run on two homicides in Red Hook, and how the head of one of the victims was amputated. The cameras caught a view of Chief Tafem and Detective Boatman viewing one of the victims in the body bag. Then and there she knew Ace got her message. At that point, Lorenzo came walking through the door.

"Hey, I stopped by Starbucks and got you a coffee just how you like."

"Thanks."

"So, what is it you needed to talk to me about?" asked Lorenzo.

"I spent three million five hundred thousand dollars with Felipe on seven grand a brick. So, I have a big shipment coming in this week. I need you to personally handle it for me."

"Now you know we are already over-stocked with what we got from Morwell," explained Lorenzo.

"I already know, so we just got to change up a few things. I'm calling for a meeting with all of the families, and all of that powder I got from Felipe we are going to let it go for fifteen thousand dollars a brick."

"Okay, I'll start making the calls this morning. When do you want to have this meeting?" asked Lorenzo.

"Set it up for tomorrow at Destiny's at three p.m."

"Okay, I'm on it." Lorenzo turned around and saw the news going off. "What's the news talking about this morning?"

"It looks like Badii's boy handled his business. He told me he would when he first told me about Masi."

"Did you do a background check on him yet?" asked Lorenzo.

"Yeah, I did that same day we met him. He doesn't have no rat shit on his name and he beat two bodies, and has been locked up for small crimes, but from what I see he's clean."

Lorenzo stopped talking because there was a knock at the door. When he got up to open it, it was Badii and Masi. Masi was carrying a book bag as he walked in the door.

"I'm taking it you have something for me in that book bag, Masi?"

Jamila looked at him as he nodded and took the book bag off. When he opened it up, he pulled Dog's head out.

"I'm glad I see I only have to ask you one time, Masi. Badii, take the bag and put it in the freezer over there with the bottles. Masi, have a seat. From this point on you will no longer dress like a thug. Your new post will be at Destiny's, and I want you there from seven a.m. to six p.m. seven days a week for your first three weeks until you get the hang of things. Badii, I want him with you, show him the ropes." Jamila opened up her top right desk drawer, and pulled out a stack of money. "Masi, this is three thousand dollars. Next time I see you, I want to see you dressed for the mob." Jamila handed the money to him. With a doubly serious look, Jamila went on: "Masi, I'm telling you like I tell everyone else who comes in this family. I will eat with you, laugh and joke with you. I will kill for you, and I will also be the one to send someone to kill you and your family and dump your bodies in the Hudson. When I lose your loyalty, you lose my trust and I take your life. Tomorrow morning, be at Destiny's."

"I will and I'll be dressed for the mob."

Chapter 10

"First, I would like to thank all of you for coming. I know we all have had our differences in the past, but that's the past." Red Invee walked around the round table as she ran her fingers across everyone's shoulders, as she passed them and talked. "I have something for all of you here. Badii, if you don't mind, please pass everyone a wrapped package." Red Invee sat at the head of the table, as Badii passed out the wrapped packages to everyone. Once he was done and standing beside her, she continued talking. "The reason I called this meeting is for new businesses on my end that will benefit all of us. What you have in front of you is ninety-nine point nine percent pure cocaine. You can cut it three times and it will still be the best product in NYC. The kilos in front of you are free from me to take back and sample. Each kilo I have is going for fifteen thousand dollars, and I will not be selling this to anyone outside of us for fifteen grand. That price is ya price. Just like I know you have your prices for others outside of us. I'm not trying to step on no one's feet at this table, but as the head Don, my job is to make sure we keep a hold on this city by all means."

"Mrs. LaCross, you do know with these prices we will have visitors from across the water."

"Let them come, Mr. Gambino. If you decide to sell each kilo for thirty thousand dollars, you will be making your money back plus fifteen thousand dollars on top of it."

"Mrs. LaCross, what I'm about to say I hope no one takes as disrespect, but you have been the Don here for two years. Within these two years you've opened up more doors for us than Tony and Chris and you don't ask for us to pay dues. Now you are selling us ninety-nine percent pure cocaine for fifteen thousand dollars a kilo. You are not just for your family but all of us. You will forever have the loyalty of the Teliono family."

"Thank you, Glen Teliono!"

"If you don't mind me getting off the topic here, but there is another business that needs to be talked about."

"And what business is that, Mr. Scott?" asked Jamila.

"You have the Senato family who has just opened up a night-club in Harlem."

"And how long has this club been open, Mr. Scott?"

"A little over three months now, Mrs. LaCross."

"And you said the Senato family?"

"Yes."

"I'll go visit them this weekend. I take it very disrespectful to move in or open up a club in our city and not come to our table and ask me to move in. Now I'm going to show them the bitch in me. With that being said, before we leave, does anyone here have anything else to bring to the table?"

Looking around, nobody said a word.

"That's it then until the next meeting."

Chapter 11

"T-Bone, come take a look at this. What do you see?"

"I see a crowd of three hundred plus people, Mr. Winston," stated T-Bone, as he looked out the window of Mr. Winston's office, viewing the club scene as people were dancing, smoking, and drinking at the bar.

"So, you really think I'm gonna let a female Don stop me from doing what I'm doing?"

"I've heard a lot of stories about her, Mr. Winston and most of them weren't pretty at all."

"We also heard a lot of stories about the boogie man growing up," said Mr. Winston, but the stories were all bullshit. People will tell you stories to make you believe a lie. To make you believe what they want, T-Bone. I used to have a lot of respect for the other families over here, but if the Lenacci family and the rest of them are going to let a bitch come and take their shit over, then that opened the door for me. Come have a drink with me to money, power, and respect. I have the money, I have the power, and I will take my respect."

T-Bone looked out the window one last time at the crowd of people down below, before walking off from the office window.

***

"I'm guessing that was them looking down from the upstairs office window, Red Invee."

"That was them, Lorenzo, I also see we have two guards by the stairs and I count four walking around on the floor. Tell everyone to get ready to make their move. Lorenzo, try to get the four guards walking around altogether. I need it clean and quiet."

Lorenzo took another sip of his drink, and walked off the table. Red Invee watched as Badii and Youngboy started to fight with each other in the middle of the club. When she saw the guards running over to them to break it up, she pulled her 9mm out of her purse, and walked through the crowd towards them with her gun tucked under her purse so no one could see it. Lorenzo was walking from the other way. All six guards were walking Badii and Youngboy to the back of the club to put them out.

"Man, get the fuck off me, I know how to walk."

"Shut the fuck up and keep it moving, coming into Mr. Winston's club with all that bullshit," the guard said, yelling at Badii.

"Man, fuck Mr. Winston."

"Yeah, we know what to do with your kind." Opening the door and pushing Badii and Youngboy out, one of the guards pulled out his billy club.

At that point, Lorenzo walked up from the side. "Bang bang muthafucker, what's good?" Lorenzo said, putting his gun to the guard's face. Badii pulled his gun out, and looked at the guard who pushed him out the door.

"Hey hey now," Badii smiled, putting his gun to the guard's face.

"Gentlemen, should we talk to your boss?"

Everyone turned around and was looking at Red Invee and Masi. Masi had two Mac-11's in his hands, ready to fire off on whoever.

"You see how easy it was for me to get you out of everyone's eyesight? If you try anything, it will be easier for me to have all of you flatlined with a snap of my fingers. Now, we are going to walk up them stairs respectfully like the gentlemen you are or you can be brave fools and die tonight." The six guards already had their hands up in surrender. Red Invee looked in everyone's face after she said that. "Good, I'm glad we got an understanding. Now let's go see Mr. Winston."

***

"You know, T-Bone, I'm thinking about moving two more clubs down here. Ladies, what you think?" said Mr. Winston.

"I think you should open them, handsome."

"What about you, sweetheart?"

38

"I think you should too!"

"Come have a seat on my lap, beautiful." Mr. Winston grabbed the beautiful female by her hands, pulled her to him, and kissed her long and hard in front of T-Bone and her friend. That's when the door opened up, and he looked up and saw Youngboy with two guns in his hands with Masi right next to him.

"Fuck up and die, Mr. Winston, think stupid and get fucked up," Masi said, wanting Mr. Winston to move wrong.

Looking past them, he saw all six of his men walking in with their hands behind their backs, and Lorenzo and Badii with guns to their heads.

"All of you on your knees—We don't want to get no blood on this nice carpet Mr. Winston has in his office," said Lorenzo.

Watching his men get on their knees, Mr. Winston stared at them and fixed his tie, standing up. Then he walked in front of his desk, and leaned against it. T-Bone didn't say a word; he just stood next to Mr. Winston.

"So, I see you are all armed, may I ask who you are?"

"I'm not the one you need to be talking to," explained Lorenzo.

"So who do I need to be talking to?" asked Mr. Winston.

"That will be me," Red Invee said, walking in the door. "You have a beautiful club here, Mr. Winston."

"You must be Red Invee?"

"Yes, I'm her and you are the man who very disrespectfully moved in my backyard and opened up a nightclub without even asking me first." She walked to the bar he had in his office, and poured two shots of brandy. She then walked up to him and handed him a glass. "So tell me, Winston, what would you do if I was to come to NJ and just open up a club? From the looks of things in here, it looks like you are selling cocaine and pills."

Taking a sip of his brandy, then placing his glass down on the desk, he said, "Ladies, as you can see, I have a meeting that just walked in my office. So, I'll have to take a rain check on our little party we were going to have. You can see your way out the door."

Red Invee looked at them as they got up and went to walk out the door. "Masi, if anyone of them females walks out that door, send them to their maker on a first flight trip. This is what's going to happen, Mr. Winston—From this point on this is my club. You will sign everything over to me. That's out of respect for disrespecting me by opening a club in NY without my blessing and moving drugs in my city. What I will do is let you walk out of here alive with your men out of my goodwill.

"And what happens if I say no?" asked Mr. Winston.

"I'll show you better than I can tell you. I'll raise my hand like this and snap my fingers like that and watch what happens."

Mr. Winston watched as Lorenzo put the gun to the head of one of his guards and pulled the trigger. Blood went everywhere as his body dropped.

"Fuck," said Mr. Winston, as he jumped back.

"Now you see what you made me do, you made me put blood on my new floor. Now I'm going to give you a chance to leave after signing everything over to me, or you and this dead motherfucker can talk about me together in the afterlife."

Red Invee walked to the chair in front of his desk, and took a seat as she waited for the paperwork for the club.

Masi walked up, and put the gun to Mr. Winston's head. "Don't make her ask again."

"Alright, alright, they're right over here in the drawer." Mr. Winston looked at T-Bone and said under his breath as he was walking past him, "I'm not going out like no chump."

Red Invee caught every word as he said it. When he went to open his desk drawer, he looked at Masi as he pulled the drawer out slowly. Red Invee jumped up. "What the fuck I tell you," she said, pulling her gun out and shooting Mr. Winston two times in the chest.

As he flipped back the chair, Youngboy put his gun to T-Bone's head.

"Fuck up and die, T-Bone."

Masi was lost. Red Invee walked to the desk and pulled out the .44 bulldog Mr. Winston had in there and placed it on the desk, and looked at Masi looking at Mr. Winston on the floor. Crossing her legs, leaning back on his desk, she said, "I could have killed you, Winston, but what good are you to me dead!"

"You know who the fuck I am? You think this shit is going to blow over or my family is going to lay down as the Lenacci family did?" said Mr. Winston in pain.

"And that's why they are all laying down from sleep they will never wake up from. But you know you are right. Tuck your life." Red Invee looked at T-Bone, addressing him in a curt tone. "T-Bone—that is your name, right?"

"Yes, it is."

"This is what I'll do, take Mr. Winston and the five men over there that are still alive, and go back across the water. I don't want to have to kill anyone else. Mr. Winston, from this point on this is my club. Don't step foot in it again. Do I make myself clear?"

"You think I'm gonna roll the fuck over and let you take my shit? T-Bone, you are a fucking pussy. If she doesn't kill you, I'll kill you my fucking self; all of you—matter fact."

"You know what? I had enough of your fucking mouth." Red Invee walked up to Mr. Winston, looked him in the eye, and pointed her gun at his face. "No! Matter fact, you're going to die screaming. Youngboy, Badii, throw him out the window."

Youngboy walked over and kicked Mr. Winston in the face as Badii grabbed his arms. Masi opened up the window, while Red Invee watched as Mr. Winston was yelling and kicking as they picked him up and dropped him out the window from the third floor.

"T-Bone, go outside around back and pick his dead body up, and take him back across the water. Let whoever know I tried to talk with him, but he chose death. Lorenzo, let them up and get their ID's and let them leave. Youngboy, bring the ladies over here to me if you don't mind."

"Ladies, Red Invee wants a word with you."

"Please don't hurt us, please don't," they said, walking over to her, shaking in fear.

"I'm not going to hurt you at all, but please don't make me come back and find you because I will kill you and your loved ones. Do I make myself clear?"

"Yes, yes."

"Good. Now give me your ID's and then you can go. Lorenzo, take Masi with you and have the DJ make an announcement that the club is closing within the next forty-five minutes. T-Bone, take your men and leave." She watched as they left out the back doors to the club. She opened up Winston's desk drawer, and started reading over the files he had in his office desk. Lorenzo walked up to the DJ booth with his gun in his hand.

"Yo, turn that shit down. I need you to make an announcement."

Looking at the gun in his hand, the DJ turned the turntable off.

"Let them know the club is closing in the next forty-five minutes. It's under new management." Lorenzo pointed up at the office window, and the DJ saw Red Invee looking down at him. "Red Invee of the LaCross family owns this club now."

Chapter 12

"Yo, Ace, you good?"

"What type of question is that, Jay Pillz? My nigga got his fucking head taken off and you want to know am I good. Get the fuck out my face!"

Ace watched as Jay Pillz put his hands up and walked back through the parking lot of the projects. Smoking his blunt, leaning against his car, he saw Taz coming up with a 40 oz. in his hand and smoking a cigarette. Taz was wearing a black hoodie and some blue jeans, with black timbs.

"Yo, peace. I'm sorry to hear about Dog."

"Good looking out, my guy. I still don't know who did it, but I know Red Invee is behind this shit, Taz."

"Word on the block says he was with Masi last. Tee saw him go in Dog's spot with him last night. She was ducked off next to the 34th building. She said Masi came back out like an hour later, holding a bag over his shoulder."

Ace paused for a second. "My nigga, you telling me Masi killed Dog?"

"I'm just saying what she said she saw," replied Taz.

"Where is baby girl at now?"

"I just passed her a few minutes ago. She's right up the block."

"Yo, show me where she's at, Taz. I need to see what the fuck she's talking about. I'll have this bitch killed two to the fucking head. These niggas act like they scared of this bitch. Man, fuck Red Invee. That bitch bleed just like us, Taz."

"Trust me, Ace, I know how you feel. But that bitch is catching bodies out here back to back."

Ace looked at him from the corner of his eye, thinking to himself this nigga is a bitch too.

"Ace, she's right over there, homie."

***

"Tee, I told you, you shouldn't have said nothing around Taz. I told you he was going to run right back to Ace, now look they are walking this way now."

"It's cool, Tasha, I fuck with Ace, and I know Dog was his nigga."

"Hey, Ace."

"Tee, what's up, beautiful?" Ace said, looking at her sitting on the stairs next to Tasha.

"So she the only person you see, Ace?" said Tasha.

"Naw, Tasha, I see you too, sexy. But yo, Tee, come chop it up with me for a second."

"What's up, Ace?"

"You was out there that night Dog was with Masi?"

"Yeah, I saw them together walking into Dog's spot. Then Masi came back out like an hour later by himself."

"Who else you told that to?"

"Just you and Tasha."

"Look, don't tell nobody else that, ma, and check this out— here goes a few dollars for your pockets." Ace pulled out three $100 bills, and handed them to Tee. "Remember, keep that to yourself."

"I got you, Ace."

"Yo, Taz, I'll get up with you, homie, I'm out—Take care, Tasha," Ace said, as he walked off.

Chapter 13

Meech ran his hand across Mr. Winston's face as his body was laid down on the table. Meech looked around at everyone in the room.

"T-Bone, tell me what happened to him," said Meech.

"We were talking and he was saying he wanted to open another club in Harlem. We walked by his desk and he poured two shots for us, then the door opened up and two guys came in, their guns out. They had five guards on their knees."

"Wait, two guys came in and had five guards on their knees, is that what you are telling me, T-Bone?" asked Meech.

"No, sir, it was all together six of them at first. Two guys came in first then two more with guns to the heads of the five guards after some dude shot one of the guards. We were caught off guard. Then a few seconds later, *she* walked in the door."

"Who walked in the door, T-Bone?"

"Red Invee."

"Wait, you telling me Red Invee killed Mr. Winston?"

"Yeah, she did, but she tried to talk with him. She wasn't disrespectful at all."

"So how did he fly out of a two-story window?" said Meech, looking down at Mr. Winston's dead body, not taking his eyes off him. He had anger in his voice, looking down at his brother.

"Meech, she told him to leave, but he went to pull his gun out and she just drew faster and shot two times. Then she had one of the guards killed."

"Reese, have his body picked up. Strips, you and me are going to pay this Red Invee a visit now. Come on, let's go."

"What about me, Meech?"

"T-Bone, I need you to deliver a message to my brother and tell him this nigga going to pay for what she did to him."

"Huh? What you mean?" said T-Bone.

Meech pulled his gun out and pointed it at T-Bone.

"Meech, hold up I tried to talk with him."

Meech fired two shots to T-Bone's chest, dropping him. "Strip and Reese, now throw him out the window and meet me downstairs. We need to get ready to go across the water."

Chapter 14

Fabio walked in Frankie's yard to the pool to see him reading the paper.

"Where you coming from?" asked Frankie.

"The meat shop."

"We need to talk, have a seat but first pour us two shots of gin."

Fabio picked up the bottle, and poured two shots for himself and Frankie. After handing Frankie his glass, he took his seat.

"So what we need to talk about?"

"The code of silence, Fabio."

"I know all about the code of silence, Frankie."

"I hope you do. Take a look at these; they were brought to me yesterday."

Fabio looked at the pictures of him and Detective Boatman outside of his brownstone. There were eight of them. Fabio looked at each picture one by one.

"Where did these come from, Frankie?"

"A friend of mine. We've been trying to get something on Detective Boatman slime ass for a while now. And it just so happened we get pictures of you and him together in front of your place early in the morning."

"He tried to push up on me with a press game, but I told him to get the fuck out my face," replied Fabio.

"There's no doubt in my mind you told him to get out your face. My thing is, these pictures are two months old. Why you ain't bring this to the table when it first happened?"

"Frankie, it was nothing, not even a five-minute conversation."

"Fabio, you know how this looks, right?"

"Frankie, I know how some people will look at it," Fabio said, "but it's nothing, I assure you that."

Frankie placed his paper down on the table outside, and pulled on his cigar, looking at Fabio.

"Let's hope it's nothing, Fabio, and you ain't gambling with your life. Keep the pictures as a reminder that this life we live is life and death. And the pictures you are holding in your hands can lead to your death. Fabio, I've seen and witnessed people getting killed behind the thought of them being rats. Car bombs set-ups, the killing of kids to get them to come out from hiding. I don't want to open up the paper and hear about you being killed or see it on the news."

With those words, Frankie walked off, leaving Fabio holding the pictures in his hand at the pool. Fabio looked at the pictures one more time in his hand, placed them in his pocket, and walked off back to his car.

Chapter 15

Jamila was looking out of her office window at the city of Queens, watching the people walking around and cars driving. When her office doors opened up, she turned around and saw Lorenzo walking in with two cups of coffee in his hand.

"Hey, Jamila, what's up?" said Lorenzo, walking to the table, placing the coffee down on it.

"Lorenzo, how are the numbers coming from the new shipment from Felipe?"

"Good, real good. We grossed forty-five percent faster, twice as fast from Morwell."

"Lorenzo, I decided this is going to be our last shipment from Felipe. Next week I'm going to see him and let him know that I know it was him who had my father killed. And to let him know I will no longer be buying powder from him."

"Jamila, I don't think it's wise for you to do that. To go down there and let him know that you know he got your father killed. That's just plain fucking stupid." Lorenzo got up, walking to the back of the office.

Picking up her cup of coffee and taking a sip, she looked at Lorenzo and said, "I know you are upset but my mind is made up, and this time I'm going alone."

"Jamila, think about what you are saying."

"I did, Lorenzo, for the past three nights, and I'm leaving tomorrow night. I'm going to see Frankie."

Lorenzo walked from the back of the office, flipping over a chair before walking out the door. He looked at Jamila and said, "Then fucking gamble with your life," slamming the door as he walked out.

Jamila knew what she was doing was gambling with her life, but her mind was already made up. When she got to Frankie's house, he already knew what she was about to say as he looked at her out the window, opening his front door.

"Frankie, please hear me out before you speak. I know what you are thinking and I know going down there confronting him may just get me killed, but it's my choice and I just want you to wish me luck and support me on this."

"Jamila, I know your mind is made up, but just think about this. Think about what you are about to do. You are doing good up here, you are the Queen Don. Just let it go. I wouldn't know what to do without you."

"Frankie, I will be okay, I promise you that."

"Jamila, you can't promise me that. Me and you both know that; but like you said, your mind is made up. So, let me help you. I have a friend down there. His name is Carlos. I'll let him know you are coming down there. Here is his number, in case you need him."

"Thank you, Frankie, and how did you know I was going down there?" asked Jamila with a puzzled look on her face.

"Lorenzo called me, and he was mad about it."

Jamila got up, hugged Frankie, and kissed him on both cheeks before leaving.

Chapter 16

Youngboy was walking through the PJ's when he saw Ace and a few of his homies posted up in the front of the building.

"Yo, Ace, check it out. Ain't that the bitch ass nigga from the other day?"

Ace turned around and saw Youngboy walking inside one of the buildings.

"Hell yeah, that's the nigga, Rock. Ya niggas strap up, we're going to clap that fool and send that bitch Red Invee our own message."

Youngboy walked to one of the apartments and knocked on the door three times, then two more times.

"Who is it?" a voice from the other side of the door said.

"Youngboy."

Locks clicked, and the door opened.

"What's rocking?" said Youngboy, walking into the apartment.

"Same shit, bricks and money," Sideways said. Closing the door, he went on: "The red bag got three hundred thousand dollars and the black one has seven kilos in it. I ain't get off this week, Youngboy."

"I'm out, Sideways. I'm about to go drop some shit off to Badii and Masi. I'll pull back up on you this week with another drop."

"You need me to walk you out?" asked Sideways.

"No, I'm good, son. I got two black bitches on me ready to bust a nut." Youngboy picked up both bags, and gave Sideways a pound before walking out the door. He pulled his phone out and called Badii. After two rings, Badii picked up.

"Yoo."

"Peace, bro, I got the good from Sideways and I'm on my way to you now."

"Peace, peace, bet dat up, I'm waiting for you now. I'll see you in fifteen to twenty minutes tops."

Hanging up the phone, Youngboy walked out the door of the apartment building, and he saw Ace and his crew outside standing around.

"What's up now, nigga? You think shit sweet? That bitch Red Invee had my hitta bodied. Ya motherfuckers thought we were going to let that shit ride?"

"Ace, fuck whatever you talking about and fuck the headless dude. You know who the fuck runs the city. Ya was playing games, and he got on the grocery list and niggas ate."

Ace pulled his gun out and made a move to shoot Youngboy. Youngboy dropped his bags and pulled his guns out, but Ace shot him in the arms. Youngboy dropped his gun as he fell backward.

Ace yelled, "Yeah, motherfucker! I got a message for that bitch Red Invee and I'll make sure you deliver it." He stood over Youngboy, and shot him six times in the chest and head. "Come on, come on, and grab the bags and let's get the fuck out of here."

Youngboy was dead and laid out on the steps in front of the apartment with his gun right next to him. His eyes were still open, looking at the sky. He never had a chance.

Chapter 17

The next day, when Jamila got off the jet, she knew there was no turning back. Felipe met with her as she got off the private jet. He watched her as she stepped off the jet. When she walked up to him, she kissed him on the right cheek as he hugged her.

"So Jamila, what do I owe the pleasure of this visit?"

"Felipe, I came to talk to you about a matter I just found out about, so is there a place we can talk in private?"

"Yes, once we get to my house we can walk the horse track and talk in private. It's a beautiful day; let's enjoy the sun."

When they made it to Felipe's house, they walked the track in his backyard.

"So Mrs. LaCross, what's on your mind?"

"Felipe, I respect you a lot, and the respect to the business we have with each other is mutual." She stopped and looked at him. "Twenty years ago you had a man killed by the name of Anthony Catwell, do you remember him?"

"Yes, I do remember that name, Red Invee. So, why after all these years did this name come up?"

"Because he was my father, Felipe."

Felipe grabbed Jamila's arm to stop her from walking. "I knew that was your father before we even met. After you killed Tony and Sammy, I wanted to know who this female was, then I heard about you and the Deniro family. So, I had a few of my people do a background check on you for me. That's when I found out he was your father. At first, I didn't want to believe it, but meeting you and talking with you just made it more possible to believe that he was your father. And to the statement you made early, you were wrong. Yes, I knew your father very well but I wasn't the one who had him killed."

Jamila looked at Felipe in the eye. "Then who had him killed, Felipe?"

"Red Invee, in this life we live we hear it and don't hear it, see it and don't see it. We even lose loved ones all the time. There's something I want to show you. Please follow me."

Felipe walked Jamila into his house, to a room where he had pictures of her father at the dog track. He also had pictures of them in Las Vegas, and a few at his house. Jamila looked at all of the pictures of her father, and was lost for words. All she could do was, put her hands over her mouth as she looked over the picture. Felipe put his hands on her shoulders for comfort.

"Jamila, the name of the man who killed your father is Jatavious Stone. I don't know if you saw the video tape of him being killed, but Jatavious is the man on the tape who had him killed. Do you know who he is?" asked Felipe.

Jamila nodded, as she was looking at the pictures of her father.

"Are you going to kill him?"

"Yes, I am."

"I will help you set him up."

"Why are you helping me?"

"Because we have bumps in the road as well. It's just I can't be the one to kill him."

"Why is that, Felipe?" asked Red Invee with a surprised look on her face.

"Because of the war it will bring in my own household. You see, he is a part of my family, and he has just as much authority as I do. You understand now why I can't kill him?"

"I do understand. So, all this time you knew I was Anthony's daughter?"

"Yes, I knew then why you were able to outthink everyone else. I will see what I can do on my end to set up Jatavious Stone, and I will call you back in a few weeks." Felipe walked Red Invee back to his limo, and watched as she rode away to his private jet.

Chapter 18

Detective Boatman walked into Red Hook, drinking a cup of coffee, looking around at the scene and everything that was going on.

"Hey, Detective."

"What we got here, officer?"

"I'm thinking a gang shooting. Black male, age twenty-seven, shot six times."

Detective Boatman bent down over the body, and pulled back the white sheet.

"Fuck!"

"Is everything okay, detective?"

Detective Boatman covered the corpse back up with the sheet, and stood up. Before he could respond, Chief Tafem walked up.

"What we got here, Boatman?"

Turning around, looking at the chief, he said, "A lot more bodies to come sir. This is Youngboy LaCross. He was part of the LaCross family, and whoever whacked him—not only did they sign their death certificate but they signed whoever was around them at the time they found him. He was one of Red Invee's top sergeants, and she's going to want blood and a lot of it."

"Detective Boatman, clean this crime scene up and get this body out of here. Let's see if we can catch the asshole that did this before she does."

"I'm on it, Chief Tafem."

Turning around and walking away, Chief Tafem pulled a pack of *Black & Mild* out of his pocket, and lit it as he walked back to his car.

Detective Boatman walked up to the EMT and said, "Hey, let's get the body in the meat wagon."

"Officer?"

"Yes, Detective?"

"Get these people back and let's clean up this mess."

Lorenzo watched from the crowd as the EMT's took Youngboy's body away. He was looking at Detective Boatman walking around and talking.

"Badii, let's go. How much work did they get off of him?"

"When I pulled up on Sideways, he said he just gave him seven bricks and three hundred thousand dollars," replied Badii. "You think it was a set-up, Lorenzo?"

Opening the door to his hummer, he looked at Badii and said, "No, it wasn't a set-up. It's just a group of niggas who got a death wish, and we are going to grant that motherfucker for them. Come on, we got to get back to the restaurant. Red Invee should be back. We got to let her know what happened."

Chapter 19

When Jamila got back to New York, she went to Frankie's house to tell him about the meeting and how Felipe was going to help her set up Jatavious Stone. Stepping out of the car, Frankie met Red Invee at the door.

"I'm glad you came back in one piece," said Frankie, as he walked up to her and hugged her. "Did you talk to him about your father?"

"Yes, Frankie, he told me stories and showed me pictures of him. He also told me Jatavious Stone was the one who killed him in the videotape I saw as a child."

"Jamila, remember Jatavious Stone is a very powerful man and I'm sure he knows by now that your father's blood is on his hands and you know that now. So, you have to think smart when dealing with him."

"Frankie, I understand, but Felipe said he is the one who pulled the trigger on the tape."

"Are you sure he said that, Jamila?"

"Yes, Frankie. He also said he knew who I was for the past few years. He found out who I was after the killing of Tony and Sammy."

"Jamila, Jatavious Stone worked his way up by betraying, lying, and killing. He is a high-ranking mason. He has his hands in everything, and can have you killed with just a phone call. When you see him, don't act different or ask too many questions. Just watch your surroundings because if Felipe knew who you are, nine times out of ten so does Stone. So, what are your plans with other business with Felipe?"

"I'll do two more shipments then I'm done. I just got to stay under him until I figure all of this out."

"How are things with you and Fabio?" asked Frankie.

"Good, Frankie, we plan on meeting up later for dinner."

"So, when do you plan on jumping the broom?"

"We don't know yet, but sometime next year."

"And how is Lorenzo handling everything now that you're not in the picture as much?"

"He is doing a great job! We plan on going over some bank statements later."

"Jamila, I'm so proud of you. It's been a pleasure watching you come up the way you did."

"Thank you, Frankie. I wouldn't be where I am if it wasn't for you holding my hand on this long walk. So, thank you very much!"

Frankie nodded at Jamila. "You had a long flight home, go get some rest. I'll see you in a few days."

Jamila got up and kissed Frankie on the cheek before leaving.

Chapter 20

Lorenzo walked into Jelani's to his office, sat down behind his desk, and started looking over some files for a moment. He drifted off to the past, thinking about Elisha, Nayana, and Isaiah, and how all three of them were dead. He loved Jamila; but now that all the wars and drama were over with the other families, he started to think again that there might be a war started over Youngboy. She was going to want blood, with no questions asked. But what he didn't like was her digging up the past about her father's killing. He said to himself he was going to confront Jamila about it and let her know his feelings about another war that could be started. He was thinking about what to say to her, when his office phone started to ring.

"Hello, thank you for calling Jelani's. This is the restaurant manager Lorenzo speaking. How may I help you?"

"Lorenzo, this is Jatavious Stone."

Looking at the clock on the wall, Lorenzo saw it was 6 p.m.

"Hey, what's up, Mr. Stone?"

"I was seeing if Jamila was there?"

"No, she isn't. She's out of town right now, Mr. Stone. Is there anything I can help you with?"

"No, Lorenzo. I need to speak with her. Have her call me on this number—470-555-2152."

"Yes, I will let her know. Is there anything else you need to tell her?" asked Lorenzo.

"No, that's it."

"Okay, you have a good evening, Mr. Stone."

"You too, Lorenzo."

After hanging up the phone, Lorenzo started thinking about all the stories he'd heard about Jatavious Stone, and was wondering why he ain't call Jamila's cell phone. After a few minutes, he cleared his mind of all the thoughts and went back to checking on all of his employee's payroll and the money the family was now making, and to see if he needed to make a drop tonight. So he picked up the phone and started making calls.

SAYNOMORE

Chapter 21

"Yo, Rock, how much was all of that shit?"

"Ace, we caught beautiful off that one seven bricks and three hundred thousand dollars. So, we're seven bricks and three hundred dollars up on a dead nigga."

"Rock and B-Loe, ya be on point; we don't know how this bitch is going to come at us. Let the streets know we got a brick or twenty-five thousand dollars on the whereabouts of that pussy ass nigga Masi. Yo, B-Loe, roll that bud up. I need to smoke."

"I just need a light. That shit been rolled up, Ace. I was just letting you talk, my guy."

Nodding, Ace said: "We ain't going to fuck with Red Hook no more. I got a bitch over in the Pinks. We're going to post up over there until shit cools down for us."

"Yo, Ace, this shit is pure, bro. It's the color pink. We can cut this shit three times and still make a killing."

"I hear you, Rock, but right now we need to stay on track until we deal with Red Invee and Masi's bitch ass.

***

Jamila was looking down at Youngboy's body in the casket. She leaned forward and kissed his cheek, then his forehead.

"Sleep in peace. I love you, baby boy."

She had a private service at Destiny's for Youngboy with just family and friends. Jamila walked off from the casket to the back of the ballroom, where Lorenzo met up with her.

"Lorenzo, what's the story of what happened to him again?"

"From what Sideways told me, he walked outside and Ace and his goons were waiting on him. He never had a chance. Before he could pull out, they shot him six times and took three hundred thousand and seven kilos."

"Lorenzo, put one million dollars on Ace's head. I want him brought to me alive and his goons killed."

Jamila watched as Youngboy's mother, father, and baby brother walked up to the casket. She looked at Badii and called him over.

"Give me the bag, Badii."

He handed her a Louis Vuitton bag, then walked back to the corner of the ballroom as he watched her walk up to Youngboy's mother.

"Excuse me."

Youngboy's mother turned around and saw Jamila standing there with tears in her eyes as she held her husband's hand.

"I just came by to tell you and your family I'm sorry for your loss."

"Thank you, Mrs. LaCross, for paying for our son's services and for your sympathy, it means a lot to us."

"No problem," replied Jamila. "I have something of your son's. Everyone that works in my family I have them put savings up just in case times like this happen. This is your son's savings that I have kept for him."

Jamila handed her the Louis Vuitton bag and as she reached for it, Jamila hugged her and told her in her ear, "That's one point five million in the bag." Before she could walk off, Youngboy's little brother stopped her.

"Excuse me, lady?"

Jamila kneeled.

"Yes, handsome?"

"Are you going to find the people who did this to my big brother?"

"Yes, I am, and I'm going to make sure they pay for it. I promise."

She got up and looked at his mother and father. Then she walked off, wiping a tear from her eye.

Chapter 22

"Felipe, nice to see you again."

"It's good to see you too, Jatavious."

"So did you talk to her?" asked Felipe.

"No, I spoke to Lorenzo. Red Invee wasn't around at the time I called her. But her clock is ticking down. I already have plans to get her killed. So, tell me, Felipe, what did she talk to you about?"

"Her father is Anthony Catwell."

"Wait, did I hear you right?" exclaimed Jatavious with a look of confusion on his face.

"Yes, you did, Jatavious. Anthony Catwell's daughter is looking to talk to you about his murder."

"So why you just ain't kill her and feed her to the pigs?"

"Jatavious, she killed Tony and Sammy and Deniro. It would be a waste to kill her. We might be able to get her to work for us."

"Felipe, I already have plans to kill her. She's in my way. So what do you want me to tell her?"

"Whatever you need to, Jatavious, she is making us a lot of money."

"Felipe, don't underestimate her. She is very smart and knows how to move. So, how long have you been dealing with her, Felipe?"

"A few months. She spent close to fifty million with us already and I hear she is very respected at the table with the other families."

"She is and I will talk to her about her father when I see her again. I'll see you later, old friend. Oh, one more thing, Felipe, does she know it was you who pulled the trigger that killed her father?" asked Jatavious.

"No, just like she doesn't know it was you who cut his hand off."

"Hey, Felipe, he knows now to keep his hands out of other people's business. Let's just hope his daughter is smarter than her father. You have a good day and I will catch up with you later, Felipe."

"I'll see you then, Jatavious."

**

Jamila and Fabio went to Sunset Park to have a picnic that Monday morning.

"Jamila, I know we ain't been around each other lately, but I have been worried about you and I want to know what is on your mind. I need you to talk to me, baby."

Leaning on Fabio, she took a deep breath. "All my life I wanted to kill the man who had my father killed and now that I know who he is, I don't know what to do. I still have dreams of my father waking me up on Christmas Day, or us at this very park feeding the ducks. I just wish one day he will walk up behind me and say, 'Don't worry, everything will be alright.' Fabio, it's not fair, it's not. I fought two wars and won, and lost three friends. Two of them I killed myself because they weren't loyal to my family. I swear I would stand on loyalty and now that I met Felipe, I know he had his hands in my father's killing. I know his blood is on Felipe's hands no matter how much he says it's not. I can feel it inside of me to the point it hurts. Fabio, when you came into my life, my past came back into my life as well. It came back looking for me. I was born into this life and never knew it until I sat down with Frankie. And he told me who my father was, and now I know who I am and what my father was."

"Jamila, listen, beautiful, I love you and I told you I had a friend of mine who is helping me out when all of that stuff was going on a few years back. She was helping me run things. She's going to run things for me out there for a while. I'm not leaving your side anymore. And I know you want that big wedding but right now we can get married and have the wedding you want later down the line after all of this is over with."

"No, Fabio, I don't know how this is going to end so I want the wedding we talked about, or we can wait until all of this is over with."

"Jamila, I'm here to make you happy. So, we can have your wedding, queen, okay?"

Jamila nodded. She and Fabio fed the ducks for a few more hours longer before leaving the park. Jamila sat on the bed at home, looking at Fabio as he walked to the shower with his shirt off. Jamila hadn't been touched by a man since she and Fabio made love the last time. When Fabio walked up to her, she saw her name on his chest, followed by a rose. No matter how hard she tried to fight it, she couldn't; she needed his touch. She stood up and gave Fabio a hug that led to a kiss. Fabio grabbed her by the waist and turned her around, and kissed the back of her neck. Jamila was getting wet, and could feel her wetness running down her leg as she moaned his name.

Jamila lifted her arms so Fabio could take off her shirt, showing her flat stomach and her pink Victoria Secret bra. He pushed Jamila back to the wall as she was looking at him, breathing hard. Fabio walked up to her, putting his hands on her waist, pushing down her thong.

"Fabio, wait, wait."

"No, Jamila, I've been waiting five long years and so have you."

He turned her around, taking off her bra, exposing her 38 DD's. Jamila grabbed his dick, and held it fondly. He moved her hand and laid her down on the bed, as he put his face between her legs, moving his tongue, going circular motions inside of her pussy. Jamila wrapped her legs around Fabio's head, and grabbed the pillow to cover her face with it as she moaned long and loud. Fabio's dick was so hard it was twice the normal size when she first saw it. As Fabio lifted her legs to put his dick inside of her, she was so tight she started to scream. He took his left arm and wrapped it around her waist, holding her as he moved his waist in a circular motion. Jamila started cumming all over Fabio's dick, as she dug her fingernails in his back.

"Whose pussy is this, baby?" asked Fabio.

"It's yours, Fabio!"

They had sex for two hours. Afterwards, Fabio was fast asleep. Jamila was sore, and she knew her body needed that badly.

Chapter 23

Frankie went by Jelani's for the first time in months. When Lorenzo saw Frankie, he went downstairs to talk to him.

"Hey, Frankie, what brings you by? Is everything alright?"

"Everything is alright. I think I would eat at Jelani's today. So, Lorenzo, tell me your specials of today."

"Please follow me upstairs, Frankie."

They sat down on the 2nd floor's balcony in the VIP section, looking over the restaurant.

"So again Frankie, what brings you by today?" asked Lorenzo.

"Something to eat, Lorenzo, and to talk with you. So again Lorenzo, what are the specials for today?"

After ordering their food and a bottle of Cîroc, Frankie looked at Lorenzo.

"Lorenzo, do you understand the game that we are playing?"

"I didn't know we were playing a game, Frankie."

"This is all a game, Lorenzo, it's the game of life and death."

"So why are you telling me this, Frankie?"

Frankie took a sip of his Cîroc, and looked Lorenzo in the eye. "Lorenzo, Jamila needs to stop going to the past and leave rocks that are buried alone."

"So, what are you trying to say, Frankie?" asked Lorenzo, confused.

"I'm just trying to keep a war from being started, Lorenzo."

"Frankie, I said to myself I was going to talk with her sometime this week about that."

"We all should, Lorenzo."

"You know what, Frankie? Let's meet up sometime this week and have a sit-down with her."

"That sounds good to me, Lorenzo. So how is business going?"

"Good, real good. I haven't seen numbers like this at all, not even with the powder we are getting from Morwell. Red Invee cut the prices down, so everyone is coming this way. Frankie, hold on one second, let me take this call. Hello?"

"Hey, where you at?"

"I'm at Jelani's having lunch with Frankie. Jamila, before I forget, Jatavious Stone called looking for you last night. He gave me his number to give to you."

"Yes, I was supposed to have a meeting with him later this week. Lorenzo, go ahead and text me his number and I'll let you and Frankie finish your lunch. Give Frankie my best wishes."

"Okay, I will and I'll call you later, Jamila."

After Jamila hung up with Lorenzo, she saw he texted her the number. Looking out the window, Jamila took a deep breath before calling. A deep voice picked up.

"Hello?"

"Hey, Jatavious, it's Jamila!"

"Hello, Jamila, I called you yesterday to see if we can have our lunch date changed."

"Sure, what would be good for you?"

"How about tomorrow between twelve p.m. and one p.m., Jamila? I truly apologize. Something came up and I have to take a flight out of state in the next few days. I apologize for the late notice."

"It's okay, Mr. Stone, how about we meet up at Jelani's tomorrow around one p.m. Is that okay with you?" replied Jamila.

"Mrs. LaCross, that will be just fine. I look forward to seeing you tomorrow, Jamila."

"Likewise, I will see you tomorrow, Jatavious. Take care."

Jamila placed her phone down on the table, and walked to the nose of the yacht, and was looking out at the sea, thinking about her father, knowing she wanted a very painful death for Jatavious. Walking downstairs, she picked up her phone and called Lorenzo.

"Hey, Lorenzo, I have a meeting tomorrow at one p.m. with Jatavious Stone. Can you make sure my office is clean and my bar has refreshments, please?"

"Sure. Well, do you need me at the meeting tomorrow?" asked Lorenzo.

"Yes, I would like you to be there. Make sure you have a power suit on."

"We are meeting with Jatavious and a few of his associates?"

"I'm not sure about his associates, Lorenzo, but we are having a meeting at one p.m. tomorrow."

"I'll be here when you get here tomorrow, Jamila."

"Thank you, Lorenzo."

"No problem, Jamila, I'll see you tomorrow."

SAYNOMORE

Chapter 26

"Tatem, what's going on with the business about Red Invee? When will the Scott family get that done because it's going on six months now!"

"I'll get on that now. I'll go visit him and see what he is talking about today, Mr. Stone."

"Good because I just found out who Red Invee's father is and you will never guess who he was."

"Who was he?"

"The boogie man Anthony Catwell."

"You got to be fucking kidding me, Stone."

"I wish, Tatem. Now I know why she moves and thinks the way she does. Her father was one of the greatest killers NYC ever knew, and whatever he had she has too! Get the videotape of the investigation when Catwell got caught up with the Feds. And make sure you take the sound out of it. I don't want any sound in the tape when I go see her tomorrow. Because nine out of ten times, she wants to know why we killed him. Tell Mr. Scott I want her killing to be loud. I want to make a point when it comes to fucking with me."

"I'm going to talk to him now, boss."

"Good," said Jatavious, walking Tatem out of his office with his hand on his back.

***

"Hey baby, I ain't even hear or feel you get out the bed. Is everything alright?"

"Yeah, that was Lorenzo. I have a meeting tomorrow with Jatavious Stone and I would like you to come with me."

"I'll be there, what time is it?"

"It's at one p.m., bae."

"I'll be ready, baby."

"Thank you, Fabio. Now I'm about to go take a shower and go out for a little while because I have a few runs I need to make myself. How far out are we?"

"Twenty—thirty minutes. We should be at the docks by the time you get out of the shower."

"Okay." Jamila walked up to Fabio and kissed him on the lips before walking off to take her shower.

When she got out of the shower, she didn't say anything to Fabio; she just left. She had so much on her mind. But what she needed to do was, get something to wear for tomorrow. She went by Career's, and picked up an outfit. All night all she could do was, watch the videotape of her father being killed. She decided to do something she ain't do in a very long time. She went to see her mother.

It was 10:30 p.m. when she pulled up at her mother's house. Her front light was on. Jamila sat there in the front of the house for a few minutes, thinking about the last time she saw her mother. They got into a big fight over the tape because she found it and made a copy of it for herself after watching it. The words she said to Jamila cut her deep.

"You are dead to me like your father is dead to the world."

Taking a deep breath, Jamila opened the door and got out. She saw nothing had changed over the past eighteen years she's been gone. Even though they ain't talk over the phone, they did email each other from time to time. She told Jamila she saw her on the news a few times and never asked Jamila for money, but Jamila made sure she put $30,000 in her bank account every month. She even bought the old house. When she knocked on the door, a little girl opened it. She was no more than seven years old at the most.

"Hello, little angel, my name is Jamila!"

"Hey, Jamila, my name is Victorious."

"How are you doing, Victorious?"

"I'm doing good."

"Victorious, is Mrs. Catwell home?"

"Victorious, who did you open the door for?"

"She said her name is Jamila."

When Jamila looked up, she saw a young lady.

"Hello, my name is Jamila, I'm looking for Mrs. Catwell."

"Hello, Jamila, hold on one second. Victorious, go back to your room and I'll be up there in a minute to read you a bedtime story."

"Okay. Nice meeting you, Jamila."

"You too, Victorious."

"Jamila, come in. My name is Symone. Your mother won't be back for a few days. I'm guessing you ain't heard that she got remarried. Her last name is Walker now and Victorious is your little sister."

"Hold on, Symone, my mother got remarried and Victorious is my little sister."

"Yes, and yes."

"And who are you?"

"I'm your sister too!"

"Wait, hun, how old are you?" asked Jamila, confused.

"I'm twenty-one, your mother never told you about me?"

"No."

"Our father had an affair with my mother. It was only one time, but that's all it took. Now I'm here. Your mother had a DNA test done before he was killed. The test results came back a week later. She said she never wanted to open the results. Two years passed when she did, and I always was in her life ever since."

"When did you find out about me?" asked Jamila.

"A few years back I saw you on the news and your mother told me who you were. Then she told me everything about you. I wanted to reach out to you so many times, but I ain't know how you would react to me. Your mother told me you were living the same life as your father and she didn't want me or Victorious around it."

"Symone, listen, this is a lot on me. I have to go."

After a pause, Jamila asked: "And Victorious's father is who she is with now?"

"Yes."

"Symone, here's my number. Call me tomorrow night some-time."

"Okay, I will, Jamila."

"Call me sis because that's what we are together, we're sisters."

Jamila hugged Symone before walking off. She thought to herself as she walked to the car: *My mother never told me she remarried.* Once in the car, Jamila looked at Symone one more time before pulling off. She waved as Symone was in the doorway watching her drive off. It was 12:30 a.m., and Jamila was still thinking about Symone and Victorious.

Chapter 27

Jamila had on an all-purple dress with four-inch heels. Her hair was pressed down with curls at the tips. She had two diamond earrings in her ear, a diamond chain, and wore a pair of Gucci glasses. When she walked into Jelani's, Lorenzo and Fabio were already in her office waiting on her. When she walked into the office, she walked to her desk and sat down. Before she could say a word, the buzzer went off. Jamila pressed the speaker.

"Hello? Mrs. LaCross, your guests have just arrived."

"Can you please bring them up to my office, Jackie?"

"Yes, Mrs. LaCross."

"Lorenzo, can you go meet Jatavious Stone at the door when he comes in?" said Jackie.

"Guess so, I believe he brought some more people with him."

Once Fabio reached the door, Jackie opened it. Jatavious Stone had four men with him, and one was holding a briefcase in his hand.

"Jamila, it's good to see you again. Looking beautiful as always!"

"You are too kind, Jatavious."

Jatavious just smiled at her.

"Let me introduce you to my friends. This is Que, Glen, Phil, and Tatem. Everyone, this is the Queen Don Jamila LaCross, her second-in-command Lorenzo, and her soon-to-be husband—Fabio. So, can I take a seat?" asked Jatavious.

"Please do so. I know why you called me to have this meeting today."

"So, I'll be blunt with you, Jamila. Me and Anthony Catwell did have ups and downs and a lot of words we couldn't take back. In this life we live, people die all the time. Loved ones, friends, and family. Out of respect for your father, Jamila—"

"Mr. Stone, let me stop you for a second. You said out of respect for my father but you sent a video of him being cut into pieces. They shot him in the back of the head. Do you know the pain my mother went through watching him get killed? The nightmares and how it haunted me to see him be tortured and killed!"

"Jamila, you and your mother were supposed to die, but I let you live because of the respect I had for your father. I know you loved him, but this videotape will show you why he had to die that way. You and Felipe are making a lot of money together. Don't let his death stop a friendship before it starts."

"Mr. Stone, how am I supposed to do business with someone who had my father's blood on their hands?"

"Jamila, you have a good point, but watch the DVD then contact me afterward. You, Fabio, Lorenzo—you have a good afternoon. I will be looking forward to hearing from you soon."

"I will be in touch, Mr. Stone."

"Jamila, I'm truly sorry we had this meeting under these circumstances."

She just watched as Jatavious Stone walked out. Everything in her wanted to kill them, but she sat there knowing his time was coming soon.

"Fabio and Lorenzo, can I have my office to myself for a little while?"

When they walked out, Jamila went into the secret office that no one knew about. She put the DVD in the player, and watched her father talking to the FBI. Her mother never told her he was an informant. From the looks of things, he had been doing it for a while, maybe even years. Thinking back now, Jamila remembered Frankie telling her that her father told Tony how much money he would be losing. It wasn't a bad deal. It was a set-up on Felipe's part; her father was trying to look out for Tony, and it was all on tape. Jamila had sat there for two hours, watching the video when the phone went off.

"Hello?"

"Hey, it's me, Symone!"

"Oh, hey."

"Did I catch you at a bad time?"

"No, I was just wrapping things up. What are you doing?" asked Jamila.

"Nothing, I was just calling to let you know your mother came home this morning. Would you like to stop by?"

"Maybe some other time, Symone. Do you have a car?"

"No, not yet."

"Do you want to come stay with me tonight?"

"For real?"

"Yeah, meet me up the block of my mom's house in thirty to forty minutes. By the way, is this your cell phone?"

"Yeah."

"I'll call you when I get close."

"Okay, I'll be waiting."

"See you soon."

Jamila took the CD out of her DVD player, placed it in her drawer, and walked out of the office, locking the door behind her. She went home and switched cars, and got into her all-white LS 500. When she got close to her mother's house, she called Symone to meet her up the block. She ain't want her mother to see her picking Symone up. When she got there, it was 7:30 p.m. that evening. Symone was standing at the corner store, talking to a few of her friends. She ain't even see Jamila when she pulled up. Jamila just watched her looking real cute talking to some guys. She was thinking back how she ain't been there in years, and how she used to love eating the sandwiches out of that store. She decided to get out. Upon stepping out of the car, all the guys looked at her as she walked up to Symone.

"Hey, sis."

"Hey, little sis, do you want something out of this store?" asked Jamila.

"No, I'm okay."

"Okay. Watch my car, Symone. I'll be right back."

Watching Jamila go into the store, Mike B pulled up on Symone.

"Yoo, Symone, that's your sister?" he asked.

"Yeah, why?"

"Why you never told me Jamila was your sister?"

"I ain't know I had to tell you."

"Your sister runs the city, everyone knows who she is."

"Here she comes now, Mike, do you want me to introduce you?"

"Not right now, Symone."

Jamila saw that everyone was looking at her as she walked out of the store, so she decided to have some fun with them to show off for her little sister.

"Hey, Derrick, how you been?" asked Jamila.

"I've been okay. I ain't know you knew me, Jamila."

"You don't suppose to know that I know you, Derrick—or you, Slim Boogie, Man and BR. As for you, Mike, I need you to call me this weekend. I see you be in Red Hook a lot. Here is my number. Call me Friday around seven thirty p.m. That's good with you?"

"Yeah, that will be fine, Red Invee."

"Symone, come on, sis, we have a lot to catch up on." Once in the car, Symone looked at Jamila.

"Hey, I ain't know you knew them."

"I know a lot of people, sis. So tell me, how was your day?"

"It was cool. Victorious told your mother you came by."

"And what did my mother have to say?"

"She asked me and I told her yeah, and that I told you everything. She was mad at first, but then she cooled down."

"Does she know you're with me now?"

"She told me to go out with you tonight to get to know you. This is a nice car, sis, what year is it?" asked Symone.

"2002 LS 500".

They pulled up to one of Jamila's penthouses. She hadn't been there in months, but she had it laced out. Two fireplaces—one in the master bedroom, a ten-foot-tall ceiling with carpet wall to wall except in the kitchen. She had a sixty-two-inch TV in the living room with white and black Ralph Lauren furniture. As they went in, Symone had a look of amazement on her face.

"Now sis, this place is dope!"

"Thanks, now tell me about yourself."

"Well, I graduated high school in 2019. I work at Foot Locker, and me and my boyfriend broke up three months ago."

"Why?" asked Jamila.

"We were together three years and he said what you won't do, someone else will."

"What he means by that Symone?"

"He was trying to get me to do a threesome and I'm not with all that. So my homegirl who I thought was my friend betrayed me. I called her one day and she ain't pick up. I tried a few more times, but when I ain't get an answer, I walked down the street to her house. Her mother told me she wasn't there. So when I was leaving, a friend of mine gave me a ride to my boyfriend's house, and his car was there. I went through the back door and when I got to his room, that's when I saw them having sex. So, the chain, the key he gave me to his house, and his ring—I left them all there. He called me and told me I had no business sneaking around his house or coming over without calling first.

"So, where is he at now?" asked Jamila.

"With Ashley still. That's her name. She tried calling me a few times. She told me she was sorry, but I'm good. I told her to keep him. He does little kid things, like, send me pictures of them together, or he may ride by me and beep, things like that."

"Fuck both of them, Symone, they have no loyalty. So, why you move in with my mother?"

"My mother died a few years ago."

"I'm sorry to hear that."

"That's why I stay at your mother's house or a friend of mine's house."

"So, what do you do with the money from your job?" asked Jamila.

"It's part-time. So, food and clothes are all I can buy. I only make a hundred and twenty-five dollars a week, give or take."

"Well, look, Symone, let's order pizza and watch some Lifetime, and tomorrow we're going to hang out. How does that sound?"

"Good, so what made you like this lifestyle?"

"That's a very long story for another night. Not tonight, sis."

Fabio had called Jamila a few times, so she called him back and told him she will be home tomorrow night. Tonight was all about her little sister. It was 2:00 a.m. when she looked at Symone sleeping on the love seat. Jamila went over some bank statements, and decided she was going to have Symone run one of her nightclubs. The next morning, she took Symone shopping and asked her whether she would like to run one of her clubs. She took her by *Passion's*, and Symone said she had been there before. Jamila asked her if she wanted the job, and Symone replied, "Yeah!"

"It pays a thousand dollars a week. Symone, look, I have to go take care of some business."

"So, you going to drop me back off at your mom's house?"

"No, I was thinking you can stay here as long as you want, and I got one more surprise for you," said Jamila with a smile on her face.

"Okay, sis, you took me shopping, got me a bomb job, and now you're telling me to stay in your brownstone."

"Yeah, now Symone, you have an all-white Lexus too!"

"Oh my God, thank you, sis!"

Jamila looked at her sister, and felt good watching her jump and down. She promised herself she was going to give her sister the world one day at a time.

"Symone, I got to make a run, the keys are on the table. I'll call you later, beautiful, remember to be at *Club Passions* at six-thirty p.m. tonight. I'll meet you up there, and don't let too many people know where you stay at. I don't want them coming for you because of me."

"Okay, I won't, sis," replied Symone.

Jamila gave her a hug and kiss before she walked out the door. She had four missed calls, one from Lorenzo, two from Fabio, and one from Felipe. Jamila called Felipe back; after two rings, he picked up.

"Hello, Felipe, I apologize I missed your call."

"It's okay, Red Invee, I was calling to see how the meeting went."

"It went good and I do honor the life and everything that comes with it, Felipe."

"That's good to hear. When will I be hearing from you again?"

"How about you come up here so we can talk, Felipe?"

"That will be fine with me. I will call you when I'm on the way up, Jamila."

"Okay, I will be waiting to see you, Felipe."

As Jamila hung up the phone, she was thinking that she had over 100,000 kilos and about 300 more coming. She was going to tell Felipe it's over once he comes. She made over fifty million dollars within the last six months, but her loyalty still was with her father and not with Felipe. He had her father's blood on his hands. Once Jamila pulled up at Fabio's house, she saw him standing next to his car outside looking shirtless and sexy in his dark blue jeans.

"Hey, baby, come on, let's go in the house and talk," she told Fabio after getting out of her car.

Chapter 28

Symone pulled up at Mrs. Walker's house, still in shock that she had a new car and her place now. Once she stepped out of the car, she saw her ex and Ashley driving by. He was looking at her get out of her new all-white Lexus. She smiled and shook her head at him, then walked into Mrs. Walker's house.

"Hey, Mrs. Walker."

"Hey, child. I see you and your sister are getting along."

"Yeah, she got me a car, a new job at one of her nightclubs, and my Brownstone!"

"Symone, I know it feels good to be hanging around your big sister, but I don't want you to get caught up in that lifestyle."

"I promise, Mrs. Walker, I won't. Where is Victorious at?"

"She's in her room."

"Victorious, come downstairs. I have a present for you."

"Here I come now, where is it?" replied Victorious.

"Right here."

"Oh my God, it's a Barbie dream house with a pink car. Thank you, Symone!"

"I ain't get it for you."

"Who did?" asked Victorious.

"Do you remember Jamila?"

"Yeah."

"She did."

"Can I call her, Symone, and say thank you?"

"Sure you can. I'm calling her now."

"Hello?"

"Thank you, Jamila!"

"You're welcome, Victorious. You like it?" asked Jamila.

"Yes, are you going to come play with it with me?"

"Not today, but I will one day. I promise."

"Okay."

"Nice speaking to you, Victorious, let me talk to Symone now."

"Hey, sis, you take care of your business?"

"Yeah, I'm at home going over some paperwork now."

"Okay, I'll see you tonight."

"Remember, Symone, six p.m."

"I will."

"Okay, bye."

"Bye."

"So, I'm taking it, Symone, you're going to see her again tonight?" asked Mrs. Walker.

"Yeah, I have to work."

"Now where is this club again?"

"Off of Avon, it's called *Passions*."

"Okay, just be safe."

"I will. I have to go now. I'll see you later, Mrs. Walker. Bye, Victorious."

Walking out the door, Symone saw Slim Boogie. "Hey, what's what, Slim Boogie?"

"Nothing, so I only have one question, Symone. Jamila really is your sister? Why you ain't never tell us?" asked Slim Boogie.

"I ain't want nobody in my family business."

"I respect that, so what are you about to do now?"

"Go get ready for tonight. I'm the new manager at *Passions*, y'all should come through tonight."

"Facts, I'll be there," replied Slim Boogie.

"Don't have me looking for you, Boogie, and you don't show up."

"Man, I told you I got you, now drop me off at the corner."

"Get in."

"This shit is fly as fuck," said Boogie.

"Thank you. Look, I'm not pulling in the parking lot because I don't want to see them over there."

"That's cool, you can pull over here and I'll see you tonight, Symone."

"Okay, Boogie."

As Symone drove off, she saw Ashley walked up to Boogie. "Boogie, who was that who dropped you off?"

"That's Symone in her new car."

"Oh, that's her car, I saw it earlier at Mrs. Walker's house but I ain't know."

"Yeah and she's the new manager at *Passions*. She's opening up tonight, you should come up there."

"I see you have jokes, Boogie."

SAYNOMORE

Chapter 29

Detective Boatman was in an alley behind a store called *Browns,* smoking a *Black & Mild* cigar, leaning against his car. When he saw the black BMW pulling up, he watched as Fabio got out of the car and walked up to him.

"You're late."

"I'm here, that's all that matters," replied Fabio.

"I got word that your bitch had Dog's head chopped off. That's why they rocked Youngboy to sleep."

"Shit! It sounds like you know more than me this morning, Detective."

Detective Boatman threw his *Black &Mild* down on the ground, and smiled at Fabio. "So, I guess you are the tough guy now, huh? Your ass wasn't so tough when your homie was getting the blocks knocked off. Where the fuck were you then when shit was hot in these streets, Fabio? So, I'm asking you again, what the fuck is going on in my damn streets that I don't know about?"

Fabio looked around to make sure no one was around to see them. "Red Invee had Lorenzo, Badii and Youngboy pull up on Ace and his crew to let them know to stay out of Red Hook. Word got back to her that Dog was still making moves over there. So, she had a new nigga named Masi put the work in on Dog. So, Ace caught Youngboy over there and got him down bad for seven kilos and three hundred thousand dollars in cash. Now there's so much money on his head his fucking shadow will tell on his ass."

"Yeah, I heard some shit like that. That's why there's a brick on Masi's head. Now the pieces of this puzzle are getting put together." Detective Boatman walked back to his car, and Fabio just watched him as he opened his car door. "Ah, Fabio, catch." He threw Fabio a paper bag.

"What's this?" asked Fabio.

"Open it."

When Fabio looked inside it, he looked back at Detective Boatman.

"Yeah, that's for you fucking rat," said Detective Boatman, as he got in his car and drove off.

Fabio threw the bag on the ground next to the dumpster, and a block of cheese rolled out.

Chapter 30

It was 5:30 p.m. when Symone made it back to her Brownstone. She went and got her hair and nails done. She got dressed and was out the door, on the way to the club. When she pulled up to the club, there was a black Benz CLK parked, and she pulled in next to it. It was 6:25 p.m. when she walked into the club and saw Jamila standing there, talking to a few guys. They all looked at her when she walked in.

"Symone, let me introduce you to your staff that work the bar. You have four bars and two bartenders that work each one. Now, these strong men are your bouncers. It's seven of them, and three of them are police officers. This is your DJ and now I have to run. I've got things I need to do. It's twenty-five dollars a head at the door and fifty dollars for the VIP. You have four VIP areas in here. It's three hundred dollars to go to the VIP upstairs next to the office. That's your office up there with them glass windows. Look, I'll be back."

Jamila walked out of the club, looked on her phone, and saw it was 7:30 p.m. That's when Slim Boogie called her.

"Hello."

"Slim Boogie, I was just thinking about you and looking at the time. Where are you at now?" asked Jamila.

"In front of Red Hook."

"I'm about to be out front in ten minutes. Be out there waiting for me. I'll be in a black Benz CLK and I want you to take a ride with me."

"Okay, I'll be out front when you get here."

When Jamila pulled up, Slim Boogie had on an all-black hoodie with some black sweat pants and black timbs. She blew her horn at him, and he ran across the front of the car to get in.

"I see you like being over here a lot, Slim Boogie."

"Yeah, I just know how to move, that's all."

"I'm glad you said that because I need you to take care of some business for me."

"What you need me to do?" replied Slim Boogie.

"About two weeks ago one of my guys got killed, Youngboy, and seven kilos are missing. I'm trying to find out where they are at. I know Ace and his crew of bitches did it, but they are MIA right now."

"Shit! I know where they are at, Red Invee. They are in a pink house, and Ace got Trap and Boy Love moving the work to stay out of sight."

"Are you sure it's them?" asked Red Invee.

"Yeah, facts. They leave every night around this time going to the southside to pick up, then they go to downtown Manhattan."

"Show me where," replied Red Invee.

Once they got downtown Manhattan, they parked on the side of the road.

"You see that spot over there? That's where they are at." They sat down there for twenty-five minutes, but there was no sign of action coming from the trap spot.

"So, tell me, Slim Boogie, what you be doing at Red Hook?"

"I just be looking out for the police, that's all."

"You don't make runs?"

"Naw, I stay clean."

"So how would you like to work for me?"

Slim Boogie looked at Red Invee. "You for real?"

"Yeah, I'll have some work for you in this upcoming week. I'll give you a call."

After dropping him back off at Red Hook, Red Invee went to check on Symone. When she pulled up, it was over two hundred people in line. She went in the back door, and right upstairs to Symone's office. Red Invee watched as Symone was talking to one of her bouncers. She opened up the glass windows so Symone could see her standing in her office. Symone looked up, and walked upstairs to her office.

"I see you have a pretty big crowd tonight."

"Now sis, you know it's always like this up in here!"

"Yeah, I guess you are right, give or take. Lil' sis, how you like it?"

"I love it!"

"Hold that thought, I think that's them, Symone. Come here, you see those two guys right there at the bar talking to those females?"

"Yeah, with the black and red on?" replied Symone.

"Yeah, have your bouncers bring them up here to me."

"Okay."

"I'll be up here waiting." Jamila walked to the bar in Symone's office, and poured herself a drink. She turned around when Trap and Boy Love walked through the door. They looked at Symone as she walked up to Red Invee.

"Trap and Boy Love, it's nice to see you up in here. I hope you are having a good time."

"Yeah, we are," said Trap, looking at Red Invee and the four bouncers who came and got them.

"Nice office."

"Thank you! It's not mine, it's hers, the lady who came and got you for me. Now, I have to ask you both something. Rumor has it that you two are moving cocaine downtown Manhattan. The crazy thing is, it's my cocaine that Ace took from me once he knocked off one of my guys. So, is it true, these rumors?"

The look on their faces gave her the answer she was looking for.

"Look, Red Invee, it was only a few times, but he never told us where the work came from."

"Trap, how long have you been hanging around Ace? Let me answer that for you, a few years now. So, that means there is no doubt in my fucking mind you ain't know that was my motherfucking shit you two motherfuckers pushing. How much work did he give you to push?"

"Just two kilos."

"So, you niggas knew it was my shit and still did the fuck shit. How much money did you two make off my shit?"

Boy Love looked at Red Invee. "Ninety thousand dollars off one of them."

Red Invee looked at her nails, and shook her head. Then she walked up to Boy Love, pulled her black 9mm out, and smacked him in the face with it over and over again until blood started running down his face. She was standing over him, hitting him as he laid on the floor, yelling in his face.

"You bitch ass niggas! Now look at you holding your face looking like a sad bitch. Who the fuck you think I am? Do you know what the fuck I will do to you, little boy? Do you?" She looked at Trap. "Now this is what the fuck you're going to do, Trap. You're going to run back to that pussy ass boy Ace and tell him I said I'm coming for him."

Trap looked at Boy Love on the floor. When he looked back at Red Invee, he saw the black 9mm pointed at him. She shot him two times, one in the leg and the other in the arm.

"Fuck!" he yelled in pain.

"Now let me tell ya this, the next time I see you trapping, I'll kill your whole fucking family and make you watch. Do I make myself clear?"

"Yeah, yeah."

"Now clean this blood up ya got on her floor. I don't care if you have to take your shirt off and do it. Symone."

"Yeah, sis."

"Make sure you close up around three-thirty a.m., maybe four, but no later than four a.m."

"Okay."

"And after they clean up the blood," Red Invee said to the bouncers that had brought Trap and Boy Love, "you two show them the way out through the back door."

"Yes, ma'am," the bouncers chorused.

"Symone, I'll call you tomorrow. Now go back downstairs and make sure everything is running smooth."

Symone looked at them on the floor cleaning up their blood with the shirts before walking back out the door. She heard stories of her sister, but she never thought she would see it first-hand. She just saw the side everyone told her about, the side Mrs. Walker warned her about. As she walked downstairs, she saw Slim Boogie.

"I see you made it."

"Yeah and guess who else did?" replied Slim Boogie.

"Who, don't tell me, Prince?"

"Yeah, him and Ashley. Everyone is up here to show you some love."

Symone looked back up at the windows to her office, and saw Jamila looking down at her. She looked back at Slim Boogie and said, "Hold on," but when she looked back at the window, Jamila was gone.

"Slim Boogie, hold on a second I have to make an announcement." Symone walked over to the DJ booth, "Hey, listen, I need to make an announcement."

"Sure."

"First, I would like to thank all of you for showing up to the hottest club in NYC, *Passions,* baby. So, to show ya some love we are giving away free drinks for one hour starting now. Enjoy ya night and thank you again for coming out to *Passions* with us."

Symone walked back over to Slim Boogie.

"Yo, this shit is jumping tonight, facts! Yo, somebody is about to pull up on you, Symone."

"Don't tell me it's Prince."

"You know it," Slim Boogie said, laughing.

"Slim Boogie, you mind if I talk to her for a minute?"

"No problem, my guy."

"Congratulations, Symone!"

"Yeah, thanks."

"So, this your spot now?" asked Prince.

"Look, Prince, we ain't cool, so I don't know why you even coming over here to me like we are."

"You know what? You're right. Let me go so you can have your five minutes of fame."

"Yeah, do that, Prince, and tell Ashley I said hi and thanks for coming to my club."

Slim Boogie heard everything, and started laughing once Prince walked off. It was 5 a.m. once Symone made it back home from the club. The club brought in $10,000 last night. When

Symone walked into her room, there was a note on her mirror from Jamila.

Hey, Symone let's have lunch tomorrow. Call me once you get in—Jamila.

Symone texted her:

Hey, I'm just now getting in from the club and it brought in $10,000 last night. We closed out at 3:45 a.m. and I can't wait to have tomorrow—Symone.

When Jamila woke up, she saw that Symone texted her. Fabio was still sleeping. He'd been flying from NY to Paris back and forth, trying to close out a deal and tie all loose ends up. Lorenzo told Jamila that Frankie and Gambino had been shopping with her now too. Jamila picked up her phone because it was ringing.

"Hello."

"Hey, Jamila, I finally got you."

"I know I've been putting a lot of weight on you, Lorenzo, from running Jelani's and working with all the baby powder. So, let's meet up tonight and talk at Jelani's, okay?"

"Sure, I'll be there at eight p.m., Jamila."

Fabio walked up behind Jamila and said, "What's wrong, baby, are you okay?"

"Yeah, I'm fine."

"What's your plan for today?"

"I was planning on taking my sister shopping again, then calling up Felipe to let him know I'm done. I just ain't figure it out how I'm going to tell him it's over. My father showed me the way by having me read two books growing up, *The 48 Laws of Power* and *The Art of War*. All my life I wanted to kill the man who killed him, but I can't because my father broke the rules. He was an informant for the FBI. And bae, it's crazy because I set Deniro up but it was different."

"Baby, fuck him and Deniro, okay? Now, do you want me to make you something to eat?"

"No, let me go text Symone back and email my mother back as well."

Hey sweetie, I just got up. I'm proud of you. Text me back! Hugs and kisses—Jamila

Jamila placed her phone down; that's when Felipe called her. "Hello?"

"Jamila, how are you?"

"I'm good and you?"

"I was calling to let you know after our talk last night I took one of my private jets up here. I'm at one of your hotels called *Destiny's.*"

"Okay, I will be there in twenty minutes so we can have brunch together."

"Okay, I will see you when you get here then."

"Fabio, I'm leaving. I have to go meet someone, so I'll see you later."

After getting dressed, she was out the door. When Jamila walked into *Destiny's,* she saw Felipe sitting at a table with a few of his men with him. When he saw her, he got up and gave her a kiss on the hand and one on the cheek.

"So, tell me, Felipe, what brings you up here so early?"

"Jamila, you have a beautiful establishment! I also went by Jelani's this morning, very classy."

"Thank you."

"Jamila, what I learned about you is that you've mastered the art of timing, but Jamila you don't always want to be on time that could be fatal one day. So try to mix it up one day and be unpredictable."

Jamila nodded at him and took in every word he said.

"So, tell me how is business going?"

"Good, real good! I'm glad you asked me that, Felipe. I wanted to let you know that this shipment will be my last shipment."

"And why is that?" asked Felipe.

"I have more than enough as of right now and I know what my father was. But, still, you have his blood on your hands and no matter what, I really can't sit tight knowing I'm working with the man who killed him."

"I respect your honesty, Jamila, but we have a deal. So, now the question is, how can we make this right and honor our word?" asked Felipe.

"I don't know, Felipe, what do you have in mind?"

"This is what I will do for you, Jamila. One last shipment at the same price plus five on top of it if I have to move it for you. And do you remember the talk we had at my house about my little problem?"

"Yeah, I do remember that talk."

"So, I'll put this on the table. You take care of that for me, and we both honor our words. How does that sound to you?" replied Felipe.

"How long do I have to handle this problem?"

"A few weeks at the most. Okay, Jamila, like always, it's been a pleasure doing business with you."

"Likewise, Felipe."

"So now, Jamila, shall we order?"

"Yes."

Jamila and Felipe sat there for the next few hours before he left. It was 12:30 p.m. when Jamila pulled up at Symone's. When she walked in, Symone was still asleep on the love seat. Jamila left and went and got some breakfast for them. When she returned, Symone was up and talking on the phone, very upset. When she saw Jamila, she hung up.

"Hey, you okay?" asked Jamila.

"Yeah."

"No, you aren't, what's wrong?"

"I'm just so sick of him. I don't text him at all and he still calling and texting my phone, saying crazy shit."

"Where is he at?"

"No, sis, it's okay."

"You sure?"

"Yeah."

"So how you like running the club?" asked Jamila.

"I love it. I had so much fun last night!"

"I'm glad you enjoyed yourself last night. Hold on, sis, let me get your money. We made seven thousand dollars on the head last night. You know what, Symone? Go get dressed so we can go shopping."

***

"This is crazy, they want fifty thousand dollars for the coat."

"Symone, if you want it, get it. Money is not a problem with us."

"Hold on, one second, sis."

Jamila saw Symone looking at her phone. She'd been seeing it for the last two hours they've been shopping. What she noticed about Symone was, she was just like her a few years ago. Always trying to brush something off.

"Symone, come here. You are my sister, so I'm asking you one time. Where is he at?"

"Albany Ave, where he is always at," replied Symone.

'Come on, we're going over there now."

When they pulled up, Prince was out there with a few of his homies talking shit, laughing, and rolling dice.

"Which one is he, Symone?"

"The one with the white hoodie on."

"Symone, go to him and tell him to stop texting your damn phone and to find someone else to play with."

"Let's just leave it alone, sis."

"Symone, go over there, I'm right here."

Symone looked at Jamila, and she ain't want to tell her no after what she did last night. When Symone stepped out of the all-black Benz CLK, all eyes were on her as she walked up to Prince.

"Look, you need to stop texting me, Prince. I'm done with you. Go find someone else to play with."

"Bitch, I been done with you. You were just some action, that's all."

"Good, I'll be that. So, now you and Ashley can have each other, so stop texting my damn phone."

"Who the fuck you talking to? I don't care who you pulled up here with. I give no fucks about who in the car with you. You better understand who the fuck I am. Bitch, you was whack as fuck anyway."

"Fuck you, nigga."

Jamila sat back and listened to every word that was said. She looked at all his boys before she opened her car door. All eyes were on her when she stepped out. They couldn't see who she was because she had on a white mink coat with a hoodie, white leggings, and a pair of Timberland stilettos. When she walked up there, it had to be ten to fifteen of his homies out there along with Slim Boogie who knew who Red Invee was.

"Symone, chill, baby girl, let me have this." When Jamila took her hoodie off, everyone started backing up.

"Prince, is it? Let me tell you something, if you ever call my sister's phone again or call her out her name, I will have you stomped the fuck out and have that piece of shit car blown the fuck up. You and Ashley stay the fuck away from my little sister and this is the only time you are going to hear my voice. Next time I'll watch as niggas beat the dog shit out of you. I'll make sure you're my entertainment for the whole fucking day. You will have a pain you will never forget. I have killed more niggas just for looking at me the wrong way. So play pussy and get fucked, Prince. Test my gangsta now and I'll show you I live the life niggas like you watch in movies."

Prince just looked at her and ain't say a word.

"Now next time you try and play my sister, you better have a team of hitters because when I send my hitters out, they bringing me heads for proof. Symone, come on, we have things we need to get done today. What's up, Slim Boogie?" asked Jamila.

"What's good, Red Invee?"

"Nothing, boo, call me tomorrow around six p.m."

"I will."

"Symone, take the keys, you can drive. I have a meeting I have to go to, so you can drop me off at Jelani's and I'll pick my car up later."

"Okay, sis, I got you."

Chapter 31

"It's nice to see you showed up, Jamila."

"I know I'm a little bit late, but I lost track of time."

"So I had a talk with Mr. Felipe and he told me you are no longer doing business as far the powder goes. How did you get out of that, Jamila?"

"Frankie, he wants me to take care of Stone for him, to kill all ties."

"Jamila, I don't think you know how powerful Stone is."

"I do, Frankie, but it's too late. I already agreed to it."

"So how long do you have to take care of this?" asked Frankie.

"A few weeks, Frankie, I told him to give me. Frankie, where you been lately?"

"I've been around, Jamila. I have been thinking about putting our two families together and make one. What do you think about that?"

"I would have to think it over, Frankie. Lorenzo, how is business on your end?" asked Jamila.

"Good, here is what we grossed last month." Lorenzo passed Jamila a piece of paper.

"These are the numbers, Lorenzo?"

"Yes, they are."

"So, Jamila, Fabio told us you have a little sister."

"I didn't tell Fabio to tell you that, but I do have a little sister and her name is Symone. She's twenty-one years old and I have her running *Passions* for me."

"Why *Passions* and not *Destiny's*?"

"Because Lorenzo, she's too young. I'm letting her live a young woman's life."

"So are you going to bring her into the family?"

"No, I'm not. I don't want her to have no parts of this life, Lorenzo."

"Jamila, she's already a part of this life. Trust me, she's going to follow your steps and be just like her big sister."

"I know, but I'll try to keep her out of it. Now can we eat, y'all? I'm hungry please."

Chapter 32

"What the fuck is going on? What happened to you?"

"Red Invee caught us down bad. She broke Trap's jaw and shot me. That's why we been gone for the last few days."

"Who the fuck this bitch think she is! She feels she's untouchable? You know what? I want her fucking head."

"Ace, you tripping real shit. Ain't nobody getting close to that bitch. You're setting us up on a death trip."

"You sound like a bitch right now, Taz."

"Ya, Ace, part my back. I'm out. That bitch put a price so big on your fucking head ya mom is going to rat you the fuck out."

"And that bitch will be laying six feet deep with that bitch."

Ace watched as Taz walked out the door.

"Boy Love, you and Trap lay low. Me and the rest of the homies are going to deal with that bitch. I'll pull back up on ya in a little while. Ya just hold tight up in the spot."

***

It was 2:43 a.m. when Symone saw Slim Boogie downstairs with some of his homies in the club. She told one of the waiters to put them in the VIP, and to bring Slim Boogie to her.

"Damn! Symone, this is how you're living now. Okay, I see you facts. You doing it big, baby girl. We don't even see you in the hood no more."

"I just been busy like hell, Boogie, how you been?"

"Good."

"So, what's going on in the hood?" asked Symone.

"Same shit, everything is everything. Niggas ain't see Prince ever since that day your sister checked him."

"What about Ashley?"

"Yeah, you see her from time to time. So where you living now?"

"I have a brownstone, you should come to check it out sometime."

"Big facts, I will," replied Slim Boogie.

"Well, you can go enjoy the rest of your night. Drinks are on the house."

"Good looking, Symone."

"No problem, Slim."

"Symone, I know you really don't care, but word on the block is that Prince is dead. I wasn't going to tell you, but I ain't feel right."

"I'll find out, Boogie."

Symone watched as Slim Boogie walked out of her office. She texted Jamila and told her to call her. It was 4 a.m. when she made it home. Once she got out of the shower, she went to lay down when Jamila called her.

"Hello?"

"Hey, sis, how did it go tonight?"

"It went well. I want to ask you something."

"What's up, beautiful?"

"You remember Prince?"

"Yeah, I do," replied Jamila.

"Have you seen him?"

"Yeah, I saw him the other day, why?"

"Because someone told me he was dead."

"No, he's not dead. I just saw him. So, how much did we pull in tonight?"

"Eight thousand dollars."

"Okay, I'll come go over the books with you tomorrow. Go ahead and get some sleep. It's late."

"Okay, I'll see you tomorrow."

Slim Boogie told Jamila that Prince was showing off a video of him and Symone having sex. So, he wanted to act like a dog and for two weeks she treated him like one. She had one of her friends visit Prince and bring him to her. After seeing the tape, she could tell it was a hidden camera, so she put him in a dog cage butt ass naked with two dog bowls, one with water and the other one with dog food. She would walk up to him and say, "Here, puppy." She would make him sit and roll over. She also took pictures of him sleeping in shit while he was crying and begging her to let him out. After one more week, she let him out.

"Prince?"

"Yes."

"I want you to hear me. If you ever try and play my little sister again, I will do this to your fucking mother. Do I make myself clear?"

"Yes."

Jamila opened the back door and let him out naked, and gave the pictures to people to pass around.

SAYNOMORE

Chapter 33

"Felipe, it's good to see you again. How you been?"

"Good, Stone."

"So, tell me, which one of these dogs you bet on?" asked Stone.

"Number eleven, are you going to place a bet?"

"Yeah. I put my money on number seven."

"Lucky number seven. So, I got word you were up here a week ago."

"Yeah, I had to take care of a little business. So, how are things going with Red Invee?" asked Stone.

"Business is business. She understands what happened and knows it's all a part of business. So, this is why you asked me to fly over thirty thousand miles to ask me a question about Red Invee?"

"I'm just making sure business is running right, Felipe."

"I'll take care of my end; you just take care of your end. As far as I could remember, I've never left a loose end. As a matter of fact, I cleaned up yours last time, Stone."

"See, that's the thing, Felipe. You are always putting your foot in your mouth and you are always forgetting how you got where you are now."

"Stone, remember who helped you along the way."

"Just remember, Felipe, who was the one putting the work in. I put myself where I'm at. Now excuse me, old friend, I have to use the restroom."

Felipe watched as Stone walked out of the booth. He then picked up the newspaper in front of him and began reading. At that moment, he was shot in the chest by a sniper from across the field, taking his breath away and making him flip over the rail on a food cart crashing on the ground. Jatavious Stone watched it all and smiled as he walked away, saying, "RIP, my friend."

SAYNOMORE

Chapter 34

Frankie was watching the news at home when he saw across the TV screen: *Breaking News. Today at South Hampton dog track Felipe was shot as he was sitting in his private booth. For those who don't know who Felipe is, he is one of the biggest drug lords of today's age. He is also known for murders, drug trafficking, human trafficking, bribery, and much more, but nothing was ever able to stick to him. After a five-year hold in the local county jail and a trial that lasted up to three months, all charges were dropped against him and he was released. He placed two lawsuits against the city of New York and won. As of right now, there is no word on his condition, but stay tuned here on Fox Five News.*

***

Jamila was watching the news as the story ran on the screen.

"What you think, Jamila?"

"Lorenzo, I know this has something to do with Jatavious Stone. This is big, Lorenzo. Look, it's on every news station."

"How long ago was he shot?"

"It says it happened one hour ago."

Jamila's phone went off.

"Hello."

"Jamila, come see me."

"Okay, Frankie, I'll be there within the hour. Lorenzo, I have to go, Frankie wants me to come to see him."

"Did he tell you what it was about?" asked Lorenzo.

"No, but he sounds like it's very important. I'll call you and let you know everything once I get there."

SAYNOMORE

Chapter 35

"Masi, you got any word on where that nigga Ace is at?"

"Badii, I don't know where that fool is at. I have been looking for him ever since he rocked Youngboy. My shells are going to rip through whoever that fool is standing with when I see him."

"Facts, hands down blood on the streets! My goons' eyes are open."

"Bang, bang."

"Badii, I'm trying to roll up, what's up? You smoking?" asked Masi.

"You know I'm putting the purple in the air."

"Take a walk down the block with me then, I need a dutch."

"Check me out, Masi, Red Invee is moving you from *Destiny's* to *Passions*. She needs you there to look after her little sister."

"Copy that. Yo, whatever happened to that nightclub we got from them boys in Harlem?"

"All I know is, Lorenzo told me they crossed over that bridge and had a sit-down with Red Invee and a few other heads and came to an agreement. Something 60/40 with Red Invee getting forty percent because she had us wack his brother. Shit, the muthafucker pulled out and she opened his chest up."

"Badii, hold up a second. Ain't that that boy Taz Ace homie?"

"Dead ass that's that clown walking into the store right there."

"Yo, post up right here, I'll go get the car. We are about to do a kidnapping. That boy done fucked up now. Hurry up. I'm right here."

Masi watched as Badii pulled up in the front of the deli. He looked to see who was standing around and watched them. He saw when Badii popped the trunk, then he pulled his .45 out and was standing next to the pay phone outside the store, acting like he was making a call. When Taz walked out of the store, he saw Badii; they caught eye contact with each other.

"You got Youngboy's blood on your hands, nigga."

Taz frowned. "I ain't have shit to do with that boy getting rocked, but shit, you pulling up like you want some smoke. Now you got it."

Masi smacked Taz in the back of the head while he was looking at Badii. Once Taz dropped down on the ground, his gun fell off of his waist and slid away from him. Badii smacked him one more time in the face, knocking him out. They grabbed him and threw him in the trunk of the car. Masi ran and picked up the gun, got in the front seat, and drove off.

Chapter 36

Jamila walked into Frankie's back yard, and he was sitting in his garden, cutting up a tomato when she saw him.

"Hello, Jamila, have a seat with me."

"Hey, Frankie, what's going on?"

"Jamila, tell me you are not mixed up in this bullshit?"

"No, but is he dead?" asked Jamila.

"No, he is alive by luck."

"Where is he at?"

"Jamila, no one knows where he is at, but me and one of his bodyguards. I had a few of my guys act like EMT's and bring him here for me. Follow me, Jamila."

As they walked into Frankie's house, Frankie walked to the left-wing, and Felipe was sitting in a chair with his bodyguard standing next to him.

"Hello, Jamila."

"Oh my God! I thought you were dead."

"No, Jamila, I had on my vest. I started wearing it a year ago every time I'm around Jatavious Stone."

"So, what now, Felipe?"

"By now he knows I'm alive, and he knows I know it was him who tried to kill me."

"So, where is he at now?" asked Jamila.

"I don't know, but I know he's going to target you now, so watch out at all times because he's not to be trusted. Now, Jamila, I need you to end this for me and kill him."

"I will."

Jamila looked at Frankie and Felipe one last time before walking off, and that's when a number popped up in her phone, one that she never saw before.

"Hello?"

"Hello, Jamila."

"May I ask who I'm speaking with?"

"This is Stone."

"Hey, I was watching the news and I'm sorry for what happened to Felipe."

"Don't worry about it, there comes a time in this life we live. I was wondering, when was the last time you saw him?" asked Stone.

"About two weeks ago, he came up here to see me. It was unexpected and it was in the morning."

"Have you spoken to him since?"

"No, I have not. Is everything okay or does this go deeper than just the shooting."

"Yes, it does, but I need to find him to see the condition he's in," replied Stone.

"So, where does it leave us because I made an investment in his company last week for five million."

"Well, Jamila, let me go over some business records and I will take care of everything that needs to be taken care of."

"Thank you, Stone, can I reach you at this number?"

"Yes, you can."

"Thank you and I will be in touch with you, Stone. Have a good evening."

"You too, Jamila, take care."

***

"So do you think she knows where he is at?"

"If she does she's playing like she doesn't, but I don't think she does. But only time will tell."

"So, where do we go from here?"

"Let's take a ride to Las Vegas to let things cool off for a while. Hold on one second and let me take this call. Hello?"

"It's my turn now, Stone." Jatavious looked at his phone and laughed.

"Who was that?"

"Felipe."

Chapter 37

"Crystal, you have a call on line one."

"I'm busy right now, can you take a message for me?"

"I told them but they said it was important."

"Tell them I'll be with them in a few seconds."

"Okay."

"Thank you!"

"You're welcome."

"Hello, yes, Crystal said she will be right with you."

Jamila hadn't spoken to Crystal in almost a year.

"Hello, this is Crystal."

"How you been, Crystal?"

"Jamila?"

"Yes, dear."

"Hey, I been good, how you been?"

"I'm fine."

"This is a surprise, Jamila."

"Crystal, we need to talk. Can we meet up on 45th street?" asked Jamila.

"Sure, when?"

"How about in an hour?"

"I'll be there," replied Crystal.

"Okay, see you then."

Even though Jamila hadn't spoken to Crystal in a year, she made sure she and everybody else got what was agreed upon when they first became members of her family. Jamila was parked in a 2001 BMW when Crystal pulled up and got dropped off by a yellow cab.

"Hey, Jamila, how you been?"

"Good and you?"

"I have been good."

"So, have you been picking up your monthly package?" asked Jamila.

"Yes, I have, and thank you so much! So, tell me, what can I do for you?"

"I have a little yet big problem with Jatavious Stone."

"Wow! Jamila, that's not a little problem at all."

"Crystal, I need you to find out all you can on him for me."

"He used to have a lot of strong ties, but a few months ago he put his hand in the wrong cookie jar and was kicked out of the committee. The one with all the big dogs is a part of. I'm talking about judges, D.A.'s, Wall Street, Jamila. He put his foot in someone's shoes who was too big for him."

"So, how long he's been kicked off the committee?" asked Jamila.

"About two maybe three months at the most. But that's not all. He's in debt to them for four point five million dollars."

"But that shouldn't be a problem for him, Crystal."

"You are right but all his accounts are frozen. Jamila, he's broke. He's playing with a few thousand, that's all."

"So who all knows this?"

"Just us of the committee. Jamila, does this have something to do with Felipe shooting?"

"Yes, it does. Crystal, find out where he's at. I need to know when he shits, eats, and fucks. Now, how long before you can get me this information?"

"Give me a week or so at the most, and thank you; because of you I got on the committee."

"And how exactly is that?"

"The bust on the Deniro family."

Jamila didn't say a word; she just nodded.

"Jamila, one more thing if you can."

"Sure, what is it?"

"I was wondering if me and some of my co-workers can have dinner at Jelani's on the house?"

"Sure, just tell me when, Crystal."

"Monday, around five p.m."

"How many of y'all?"

"It's eight of us."

"Your table will be waiting on you."

"Thank you, Jamila!"

"You're welcome, Crystal, and I will give you a call next week for the information."

"I'll have everything waiting for you."

After dropping Crystal off at the subway, Jamila went home to think about everything.

Chapter 38

Symone went by Mrs. Walker's house to see her and Victorious. It's been two weeks since the last time she saw them. She saw Slim Boogie at the corner store, and decided to talk to him for a minute.

"What's up, Slim Boogie?"

"What's up, stranger? How you been?"

"Good. What's been going on around here?"

"Same shit, so I guess you ain't heard?"

"Heard what?"

"Prince was around here showing everyone a tape of y'all fucking. He had a camera hidden and he recorded it."

"Are you for real?" asked Symone.

"Yeah."

"I'mma kill him! Where he at?"

"Hold on, baby girl, ya sister took care of it already."

"What you mean?"

"She put him in a dog cage for two weeks and made him eat dog food. She put a dog tag around his neck and all. Had him butt ass naked in there sleeping in his piss and shit."

"Oh my God! She did that to him?"

"Yeah, facts. Ask Mike. He's over there talking to Alisha. Walk with me over there, come on."

"What's up, Mike B?"

"Oh shit, look what the wind blew in. How're you, lil' mama?"

"Good, how you been?"

"Mike, I'll talk to you later and you too, Slim Boogie."

"Alright, Alisha."

"So what brings you around here?" Mike asked Symone.

"I was coming to see my little sister and step mom. So, what's this I hear my sister did?"

"You told her, Slim?"

"You know I did."

"Homie was playing you, and big sis put him in his place."

"Mike showed me a picture of Prince in a dog cage eating dog food out of a dog bowl."

"What's Alisha's problem?" asked Symone.

"She thinks that it was fucked up what your sister did."

"But it's okay for him to be showing us having sex?"

"I feel you, true story."

"So, where Prince at now?"

"Shit! Old boy moved to Boston with his family."

After talking to them, Symone saw her little sister and Mrs. Walker for a few hours, then she went home and saw Jamila's car out front.

"Hey, sis."

"What's up, how long you been here for?"

"A few hours or so, where you been?"

"I went to see Mrs. Walker and Victorious. I saw Slim Boogie and Mike out there too."

"And how are they doing?" asked Jamila.

"Good. Jamila, why you do that to Prince?"

"He was acting like a dog, so I treated him like a dog. I wanted to kill him, but I didn't. Are you mad?"

"No, I just ain't never have a big sister. I'm glad I do now."

"And I'm glad you're in my life too! So, let's order a pizza and watch a movie."

"Cool. Hey, do you mind if I have a friend over?"

"Baby, this is your place. That's up to you. Who were you planning to have come over?" asked Jamila.

"Just Slim Boogie, maybe."

"It's cool. Just remember what I told you, okay?"

"I got you."

It was around nine o'clock that night when Jamila left. She called Lorenzo to ask him what he thinks about Frankie wanting to bring their families together.

"Hey, Lorenzo."

"What's up, Jamila?"

"What you doing?"

"Just cooling it."

"So, what are you thinking about bringing our families to-gether with Frankie's?" asked Jamila.

"Hey, Jamila, where you at?"

"Driving down 110."

"Come to my house."

"I'll be there in about ten minutes."

When Jamila pulled up to Lorenzo's house, he was outside talking on the phone. When he saw her pull up, he hung up and walked to her car.

"So, what's up, Lorenzo?"

"I just wanted to talk to you face to face, come inside and why are you driving alone this time of night?"

"Lorenzo, trust me, I'm good." Jamila looked around once they were in the house.

"I like what you have done in here, Lorenzo."

"Thanks, Jamila, have a seat on the sofa. So Jamila, I been going over the gross incomes from every business and it's in black and white. Jamila, we made more money from the powder in three months than we did in one year from all the businesses together."

"So how much, Lorenzo?"

"Fifty million dollars from the powder and twenty-three million dollars from all the other businesses. Now the powder we got from Morwell is still sitting in the warehouse untouched."

"How much is it all together?" asked Jamila.

"I haven't done a full count on it yet, but let me tell you—I put twenty-three million dollars in the homegrown account. If we keep moving like this, we are going to make two hundred million dollars a year, give or take. Jamila, I don't see any point in joining up with Frankie. And it's funny how he wants to join up with us and Fabio wants to marry you now. It just doesn't feel right, Jamila. You told me Fabio had someone in Paris, so why he keeps going back and forth out there so much? Jamila, you did it. Everyone is buying from you!"

"No, Lorenzo, we did it, me and you. I went to Frankie's house to talk about what we saw on the news about Felipe. When I got there, we talked for a few minutes and that's when he told me

Felipe was there. So, we went to his living room and Felipe was sitting in a chair looking out the window. Long story short, he asked me to end this for him. So, I called Crystal and that's when I found out that Stone is in hot water and all his accounts are frozen."

"So, how are you going to handle it? You want me to put someone on it? I'll have him killed within seventy-two hours."

"No, Lorenzo, I want to be the one who kills his ass. This is personal and I want his blood on my hands. I want him to feel the same pain my father did before he killed him. Have him set up, have a few girls drug him then bring him to me."

"Where is he at?" asked Lorenzo.

"I don't know, but I will find out by the end of the week."

"Once you find out let me know and I'll take it from there."

"Okay, I will, Lorenzo and it's late. Let me get going."

"Do you want me to follow you?"

"No, I'm good. I'll see you tomorrow at Jelani's."

Jamila smiled as she waved goodbye to Lorenzo while listening to Mary J. Blige and drove off. She looked at her phone, as she stopped at the red light. She ain't pay no mind to the black SUV that pulled up on the side of her.

"Yo, Ace, ain't that the bitch Red Invee right there?"

"Dead ass that's her, roll your window down, she a dead bitch tonight."

When Jamila looked up, she saw the gun, but it was too late as bullets started flying through the window. Dropping her phone, she took off driving, doing 120mph, trying to get away from them. It was three cars chasing her and shooting at her as she tried to get away. She was about to cross the Hudson Bridge when she was side-swiped, and lost control of the car. The car hit the guard rail, and that's when her head hit the steering wheel and blood started coming from her forehead. When she looked up, she saw three guys walking her way.

"I told ya this bitch bleed just like us. Now, look at her ass about to take a trip with Youngboy. Boy Love, shoot her in the face."

Jamila had her hand on her gun as she watched them get closer and closer to her.

"Yo, Ace, we should bring her back and rape her ass."

When Boy Love turned around, Jamila shot him one time in the chest.

"Shit! Ram the car, ram the car!"

The SUV rammed the car so hard it went over the bridge nose down into the Hudson with Jamila inside. The impact of the car hitting the water knocked her out.

"Damn! Boy Love. Yo, pick his body up and come on before the police come. We need to get the fuck out of here."

"Yo, Ace, you think she dead?"

"Trap, that bitch is dead. Now come on, homie." Ace looked over the rail to see Jamila's car being swallowed up by the Hudson.

SAYNOMORE

Chapter 39

"Lorenzo, you seen the news?"

"Frankie, I saw the news, I don't believe it. She can't be dead, she can't be. She was just at my house. I talked to her and she told me she will call me tomorrow morning. This shit ain't real, it ain't. Fuck, man! Fuck."

"I know how you feel, Lorenzo, I do. I loved her as my child, but we need to face the facts of reality. When they pulled the car out of the water, it had thirty bullet holes in it. They've been dragging the Hudson for six hours now and her body ain't been found."

"Frankie, that's how I know she's alive."

"Lorenzo, they found blood, her blood in the car along with her phone and gun. Lorenzo, it was late last night and her body might be miles away. Just prepare for the worst is all I'm saying."

"Hold on one second, Frankie, I got a phone call. Hello?"

"Yo, Lorenzo, I got some good news."

"What? You know where Jamila's at?"

"No, I don't know where she at. I was going to tell you we got one of Ace's boys—Taz. We kidnapped his ass yesterday."

"Where you at?" asked Lorenzo.

"The waste plant."

"Hold him. I'm on the way now."

"Bet dat up."

"Frankie, I got something to go take care of right now. I'll have to catch up with you later after I go talk to Jamila's little sister."

"Lorenzo, I don't know who just called you, but you should go talk to her sister first then go take care of whatever."

"You're right. I'll call you tomorrow, Frankie."

"Lorenzo, everything's going to be okay."

"Frankie, I never thought of how it would be without Jamila. She is my strength no matter what. She always knows how to handle anything. She never looks worried and she never shows what's too heavy on her shoulders."

"Lorenzo, go, and call me tomorrow."

"I will, Frankie."

It took Lorenzo thirty minutes to get to Symone's house. He kept having flashbacks of him and Jamila laughing with each other. Having shoot-outs side by side with each other. She was more than his friend, and even had they been blood relatives, it couldn't have made them closer to each other. No matter how hard he tried, he couldn't hold his tears back. When he pulled up to Symone's house, he looked around before knocking on the door.

"Who is it?"

"Lorenzo." He heard her opening the door. "Hey, do you know who I am?"

"No, I don't."

"My name is Lorenzo."

"Okay, you're my sister's friend."

"Yeah, I am. Do you mind if I come in?" Lorenzo asked.

"Sure, come on."

"Symone, do you know why I'm here?"

"No."

Looking at Symone, she looked just like Jamila, just a younger version.

"Lorenzo, why are you here and where is my sister at?"

"Symone, I don't know where your sister is, but let me see your remote control."

As Symone passed him the remote, he saw the confusion on her face. Turning to the news, Symone saw Jamila's car and all the bullet holes in it and how they pulled it out the Hudson.

"Lorenzo, no, no, don't tell me they killed my sister. No, don't tell me that, Lorenzo. Don't fucking tell me that, no, no!"

"Symone, I don't know."

Lorenzo held Symone as she fell to the floor, crying.

"Symone, we are going to find her, we are. Listen, I know you are hurt, but I have to go take care of something right now. Are you going to be alright?"

"Lorenzo, can I go with you?"

"I really don't want you to, not right now."

"If you don't let me come, I'm going to hit the streets and see what I can find out on my own, Lorenzo."

"You are just like your sister. Damn, come on, go get dressed." No matter how hard he tried not to look at it, the truth of the fact was, Symone really never got a chance to know her big sister and she hoped she might now get that chance to know her.

"So, where we going, Lorenzo?" asked Symone.

"Badii and Masi kidnapped one of Ace's homies."

"Who's Ace?"

"Someone who is a dead man when we find him. He killed Youngboy, one of your sister's hittas."

Symone looked around as they pulled up at Sharese Industrial Park Waste Plant.

"What is this place, Lorenzo?"

"One of your sister's spots. Now Symone, when you walk in this door, it's no turning back. I'm letting you know now."

"I'm ready, Lorenzo."

Badii and Masi had Taz tied to a steel chair in just his boxers when Symone and Lorenzo walked in.

"Lorenzo, what's up?"

"Shit! Symone, this is Badii and Masi. Yo, this is Symone, Red Invee's younger sister."

They both looked at her and threw their head up at her.

"Lorenzo, why you asked me did I know where Jamila was?" asked Badii.

"Badii, last night her car got shot up and no one has found her body yet, but the police have her phone and gun. There was blood in the car and we don't know if she is dead or alive. They fished her car out the Hudson River, but we will talk more about that later. Who is he?"

"This bitch ass nigga name is Taz and he's one of Ace's boys."

Lorenzo walked up to him and kneeled in front of him.

"Look, I'm asking you one time and one time only, where is Ace at?"

In Taz's heart, he knew he was going to die.

"Man, fuck you, I ain't telling you shit."

"That's cool with me, big facts. Masi, you ready to put some work in?" Lorenzo walked up to him and passed him a switch blade. Symone just watched as Masi took his coat off, laid it on the table, and walked up to Taz.

"Yo, where the fuck is Ace at, dog?"

"With your mother's pussy."

Masi bit his bottom lip as he rammed the knife in Taz's stomach. "With my mother, right, bitch? Now I'm showing you how I'm going to fuck you over now, pussy."

Taz was screaming out in pain, then he spoke through clenched teeth: "Nigga, that shit doesn't hurt bitch none, fuck that shit."

Masi took the knife and hit him two times in the back. Taz fell over still tied to the chair, breathing hard. Masi started kicking him in the face.

"Chill out for a minute, baby boy," Lorenzo told him.

Symone looked at Badii smoking a *Black & Mild*, watching everything and not saying a word.

"Now let's try this again. Taz, where the fuck is Ace?"

"I'd rather die with honor than die a snitch, motherfucker."

"You going to die in pain tonight, pussy."

"Yo, Masi, beat this muthafucker till he bleeds out."

"I got something else I want to do if it's cool with you, boss?" asked Masi.

"As long as this fool die in pain, do you."

"Okay, hold up, I'll be right back, Lorenzo."

Lorenzo turned around to see Symone looking at him.

"Yeah?"

"So, he got something to do with my sister's car getting shot up?"

"No, he doesn't, but his crew might."

Symone walked up to the table and picked up the same bloody knife that Masi had, and walked up to Taz. Lorenzo and Badii just watched.

"I want all ya motherfuckers to suffer for the blood of my sister y'all spilled."

Taz looked up at Symone as she took the knife and stabbed him three times in the face back to back.

"You're going to die, motherfucker, I hate ya, ahhh!"

Symone yelled until Lorenzo pulled her off of him. Taz was shaking out of control as blood was pouring out of his face.

"Calm down, Symone, he's going to die, baby girl."

Badii sat down in a chair, still not saying a word as he watched Masi coming back in with a gallon of gasoline in his hand and a sick look on his face.

"See, niggas beating you or shooting you is an easy death. I want to hear you screaming for your life. I want to see you cry, tough guy."

"Symone, you sure you want to see this? You can turn your head if you want."

"No, Lorenzo, I want to see the whole thing." Symone watched as Masi poured the gas all over Taz, talking shit as he did it.

"Man, not like this, just give me a bullet—Keep it in the streets, the g code," replied Taz in pain.

"Nigga, ain't no way we keeping it in the streets."

Masi looked at Lorenzo. Lorenzo nodded and that's when Masi dropped the match on him, and Taz's body went up in flames. Taz was screaming and making the chair jump as he tried to put himself out. Lorenzo looked at Symone and handed her his gun. Without saying a word, she walked up to Taz as he was screaming, and shot him in the head point-blank range three times, killing him. Symone just looked at his body still on fire before she walked back to Lorenzo.

Chapter 40

It's been four days and there still wasn't any word from Jamila and no body found. It started to sink into Lorenzo that she might be dead. He wasn't in his right state of mind no matter how hard he tried to pull himself together. Fabio lost it so bad that Frankie sent him back to Paris for a while. After forty-eight hours, they decided to call off the search for Jamila's body. He was looking at his laptop when he got an email.

Lorenzo, we need to talk. Meet me in Queens by the phone booth at 4 p.m. I'll have on a green coat and a pair of fishing boots. If you are not there by 4 p.m., I'm leaving—

Lorenzo looked at the time; it was 3:20 p.m. The end of the email said: *It's about Jamila.* Lorenzo ran downstairs to his car, and pulled off in traffic. He made it there within twenty-five minutes. When Lorenzo pulled up, he saw an old white man with a green coat and fishing boots. After looking around for a few minutes, Lorenzo walked up on him.

"Hey, you sent me an email?"

"Are you Lorenzo?"

"Yeah, I am."

"How do I know that?" asked the old man.

"Look, I don't have time for games, old man."

"Likewise. I have to ask you one question."

"You said it was about Jamila, not no damn question."

"Answer the question for the sake of Jamila."

"What is it?" asked Lorenzo.

"When did you tell Jamila it was Elisha who did it?"

"Where is she?"

"First answer the question."

"The night I got Miss Simpson I told her."

"Follow me then."

"Who are you?"

"A friend of Jamila's."

"How are you her friend and I don't know you?"

"Look, it's not important that you know me. What's important is that we both know Jamila, and to keep her safe. Now, we don't need to talk no more."

They walked two blocks then took a bus to southside Queens to an apartment downstairs. When he opened the door, Lorenzo saw Jamila on a sofa. She had black and blue marks on her forehead. Her arms were wrapped, and so was her leg as well.

"Jamila?"

"Lorenzo?"

"I knew you weren't dead."

"I would have been if it wasn't for Mr. Oldham."

"What happened?" asked Lorenzo.

"All I remember was leaving your house and Symone calling me and then I was getting shot at. Then I saw someone walking up to me and I shot him. Everything else after that went black. I woke up here two days ago. I been in and out and today is the first day I have been up all day. My body is super sore right now."

"Mr. Oldham, thank you for saving her life, but what exactly happened?" asked Lorenzo.

"My job is to clean up the trash in the Hudson. I was talking a break and pulled the boat under the bridge for a little while. I was drinking some coffee, that's when I heard gun shots and then a loud boom. Then I saw a body floating up the water, so I rushed and pulled her up on the boat. I did CPR on her. A few seconds later she spit up water. I knew she would be fine. Then I waited about twenty minutes before I called the police. I didn't know who them guys were. I ain't know what to do so I hid her in the bed of my boat. When it was over, I brought her here. I know a little about first aid. She didn't have any broken bones, so today when she woke up she asked me to email you and told me what to ask you to make sure it was you."

"I promise you will be rewarded for this."

"I don't need anything. I did it because it was the right thing to do."

"Thank you, Mr. Oldham. Jamila, everyone thinks you are dead. Let's get you home because we don't know who did this."

"Take me to Symone's house. I'll be safe over there."

SAYNOMORE

Chapter 41

Symone drove around the city for the past few days, hoping to hear something about her sister's shooting. She pulled up at Red Hook and the 40 projects, then went to Lincoln Ave. When she saw Boogie on the block, she pulled over to talk to him for a minute.

"Symone, what's good, beautiful?"

"Shit, get in, Slim."

"For real I'm sorry to hear about your sister. They have been talking it all week."

"Who been talking about it?" asked Symone.

"You know the streets talk."

"So, what do you know?"

"That Boy Love is dead, your sister shot him in the chest right before Ace rammed his truck into her car, pushing her off the bridge. They say they were coming back from the strip club and saw her car and pulled up next to her and Boy Love started shooting at her. It's so many stories about that shit."

"What the fuck! Them fuckboys are dead. Where are they at now?"

"Ace is in Red Hook, I know that for a fact, but I don't know where Trap is at."

"You hungry, Slim Boogie?"

"A little bit."

"Okay, we're going to go to my house and order some food to eat."

When they pulled up at Symone's house, she saw Lorenzo's truck there.

"Look, don't talk too much. My sister's second-in- command is here." When Symone opened the door, Lorenzo, Badii, and Masi were standing there. Masi and Badii had their guns in their hands.

"Symone, who is this?" asked Lorenzo.

"Slim Boogie."

"Lorenzo, it's okay, I know him."

When Symone heard Jamila's voice, she pushed Lorenzo to the side and ran to give Jamila a big hug. She had tears in her eyes.

"I'm so glad you made it, I thought you were dead."

"Don't worry, baby girl, it's gonna take more than three cars and a few fake ass thugs to kill me."

"Look at your face, oh my God!"

"Symone, I'm okay. Lorenzo told me what you did. Are you sure you want to live this life?"

Symone looked at Jamila and then Lorenzo, Badii, and Masi.

"Jamila, I killed him. There's no turning back for me now, so yes."

"Symone, just because you are my sister, don't think I'm going to go light on you. I want hundred percent at all times."

"And I'll give you that, sis."

"Good, now we need to find out who tried to kill me."

"I know who did, I found out."

When Symone said that, all eyes were on her.

"Symone, you know who tried to kill your sister?" asked Lorenzo.

"Tell them, Slim Boogie, tell them what you told me."

"Slim Boogie, come here."

"I'm glad you good, Jamila, three cars and a truck rammed you off the bridge into the Hudson and you're still here. You tough like Barbie!"

"Thanks, now tell me who did this, who tried to kill me?" asked Jamila.

"It was Ace. They saw you when you were coming back from wherever you were coming from. You killed Boy Love before you went off the bridge."

"Where is Ace at now?"

"Red Hook and we don't know where Trap is at."

"Slim Boogie, don't let no one know you saw me."

"That's my word, I won't."

"Lorenzo, give him a few hundred for me. Symone, drop him off at Red Hook. Boogie, keep an eye out for me over there and let me know who over there with Ace."

"Okay, I got you, Jamila."

"Badii, you and Masi go to the hardware store and get me a machete. It's time to put blood in the streets. Symone, come back here. We are going over there together. Lorenzo, let me use your phone to call Frankie. Hello, Frankie."

"Jamila, thank God you are alive. What happened?"

"Someone tried to kill me, but I'll take care of that in a few minutes. I'm calling to let you know I'm coming to see you in the morning."

"I'll be waiting, Jamila."

"I'll see you then, Frankie. Here you go, Lorenzo. I'll make this motherfucker pay in front of everyone. I'll show him what happens when you cross the LaCross family."

When Jamila pulled up to Red Hook, Lorenzo, Badii and Masi stepped out of the Range Rover. Symone pulled up behind them and walked on to Slim Boogie. She had on a long bubble coat so you couldn't see the gun on her waist. Badii and Masi walked up to Ace and his crew rolling dice. They ain't see them because they had their hoodies on. Badii and Masi were behind them and Symone was watching everything from where she stood.

"Come on, ya know who run shit. I run this dice game in this hood. Bitches and niggas in the game know I'm second to none!"

Masi looked at Badii and shook his head. "Yo, Ace, you don't run shit." When he looked up, Masi shot him in the arm then Badii pulled out his gun.

"Anyone of ya niggas move, you going to fuck up and die."

Lorenzo walked from behind Badii and Masi, and looked at Ace.

"So, you know you fucked up, right?"

Symone and Slim Boogie walked up to where Lorenzo was standing. Symone had her gun out when she walked up.

"You try to run, I'll put a hole in your fucking head."

"So, what the fuck you waiting for? You going to kill me, then kill me. I give no fuck, I put that clown Youngboy in the ground and that bitch Red Invee. So, it's a win-win for me. Queens is going to know who the fuck I am."

Everyone looked when they saw a female walking up slow with a black fur coat on with a hoodie. She had a machete in her hand, as she walked up to him. Ace looked at her walking up.

"You mean that bitch Red Invee?" One could tell Jamila's leg was still in pain as she walked. Ace's eyes got big as hell.

"Man, fuck that! All ya niggas, get on your knees," Masi yelled.

Red Invee watched as all of them did what Masi said.

"So you tried to kill me, Ace?"

"Fuck you, bitch, you got all these pussy niggas scared of you, but I'm not.

Lorenzo pulled his gun out and smacked Ace in the face, dropping him to the ground. There had to be fifty or more people out there watching everything. Red Invee looked around at everyone standing around looking at them. Lorenzo grabbed Ace's arm, Slim Boogie grabbed his other arm. Ace tried to fight Slim Boogie and Lorenzo when they grabbed him, but Symone smacked him in the face with the gun, taking the fight out of him. After grabbing him, Jamila said out loud, "If I see a videotape or have a detective come looking for me, I swear I'll have your whole fucking family killed, try me."

Ace looked at his boys with blood coming down his face. Ace turned around just as Red Invee was coming down with the machete, taking his arm off. Blood went everywhere as Ace was screaming. Slim Boogie let his other arm go, and looked at Red Invee. She swung one more time, and took half his face off, and kept on until she cut his head right off. Everyone was looking at what she was doing. Ace's body was shaking out of control, just jumping. Red Invee was in pain and breathing hard.

"Badii, Masi, and Symone kill all of them."

"What, what—" Ace's goons began, but they were cut short by blazing guns. *Boom! Boom! Boom!* Their bodies dropped.

"If I get court date, ya family will have a face to face conversation with their maker," Jamila said to the onlookers.

All four of them walked off, leaving Ace and his boys dead in the middle of the projects.

"Badii, you and Lorenzo take Slim Boogie to the waste plant. Symone, you and Masi are coming with me."

Slim Boogie looked confused, but ain't say anything; he just went. Symone watched as Slim Boogie got in the car and drove off with Lorenzo and Badii while she, Jamila and Masi drove off as well.

"Sis, you did that in front of everybody. You don't think they going to call the police?"

"Symone, I have fairs at Red Hook. I help rent there for those who can't afford it. I help with the children's school supplies as well as put food on everyone's table that comes to me in Red Hook. What I can say is, they see it and don't see it and hear it and don't hear it. That's why I chose Red Hook as my trap."

"I understand, but why is Slim Boogie going to the waste plant?" asked Symone.

"Because he dropped the ball. He let Ace's arm go, so I'll have a one on one talk with him. Don't worry, he's going to be just fine."

Jamila looked out the window as Masi drove through the city, knowing she just made a point as regards what will happen to you when you fuck with the LaCross team.

SAYNOMORE

Chapter 42

Detective Boatman walked into Red Hook, and was just looking at the mess that was standing in front of him.

"I knew this was going to happen." As he looked around, he saw over one hundred people standing around watching everything when his phone went off.

"Hello?"

"Boatman, what we got out there?"

"From what I can tell, Chief Tafem, she found out who killed Youngboy, and she made sure they knew what happens when you fuck with the LaCross family. It's horrible out here. Four killed, one chopped up head, arms. It's ugly."

After a pause, Boatman asked: "Did anything come back on her gun?"

"No, Boatman, the gun was clean and her lawyer called to let it be known she was alive. They had the whole thing dressed up."

"So, what now, sir?"

"Just do what you can out there and I'll see you when you get back to the station."

"Copy. Officers, come here."

"Yes, detective."

"Let's wrap this up."

"You not going to try and see what happened out here?"

"Shit, I know what happened out here. Four motherfuckers got killed and they made a point out of one of them. These people ain't going to say shit. Me trying to find out is like looking for a needle in a haystack. Get the victims' names for me. Have them bagged up and let's get on with the rest of our fucking day. She's doing it. Jamila LaCross aka Red Invee is becoming untouchable. She has these people's respect. They fear her. Let me show you something, officer, watch this.

"Excuse me, miss. My name is Detective Boatman, may I have a word with you?"

"No, you may not. Have a good day, snitch!"

Detective Boatman looked at the officer. "You see what I mean. It's pointless. It's just another day in Brooklyn. Now again let's wrap this up."

Chapter 43

When Jamila pulled up at the waste plant, she saw Lorenzo's Range Rover out front.

"Symone, you and Masi follow me. Once I go talk to Slim Boogie, I want Badii to show ya around."

"Okay, sis."

Symone looked lost as to what Jamila just said, knowing how Jamila is. Slim Boogie was sitting in a chair, looking at Badii and Lorenzo, not saying a word. When the door opened, everyone looked at Jamila when she walked in.

"Lorenzo, you stay. Badii, show Symone and Masi the plant."

Badii got up and walked out the door. Symone looked at Slim Boogie one time before leaving. Jamila took her coat off and laid it on the back of the chair before she sat down, and looked at Slim Boogie.

"Slim, I need you to be truthful with me."

Slim Boogie nodded at Jamila.

"Do you want to be a part of this life I live? Because I can open doors no one can close. I am the queen of the city, but in this life, death comes for you at every door and there is no turning back. Niggas only respect violence. So are you sure you want this life?" Jamila asked.

"Jamila, with the utmost respect I understand the life you live and I know I'm ready to be a part of it. And I also know that I'm sitting in this chair because I fucked up and let Ace's arm go, but I won't drop the ball again."

"Good, Slim, because you only get one fuck up with me and only one. Now I'm not going to look at that as a fuck up because you are not a part of this family yet, but you will have to put blood on your hands to be a part of this family."

"Okay, I understand and I will do what I need to do."

"Good because the next job I need done is on you."

Slim Boogie nodded. Jamila stood up, walked to Slim Boogie, and gave him a kiss on the forehead.

SAYNOMORE

Chapter 44

It was 6 a.m. when Jamila got a call from Crystal. Jamila looked at her phone.

"Hello."

"Good morning, Jamila."

"Hey, Crystal, why are you up so early?" asked Jamila.

"I heard what happened to you. Are you okay?"

"Yeah, I'm good, Crystal. Thanks for checking on me."

"No problem. I just emailed you everything I have on Jatavious Stone and it's a lot, Jamila. I also found out he's in Las Vegas at the Branch House Hotel Room 212."

"Thank you, Crystal, and I'm sorry for not being able to host you and your co-workers. But how about this upcoming week? I'll have a table ready for ya, how does that sound?"

"That sounds good to me!"

"Okay, I look forward to seeing you then."

"Thanks, Jamila."

"You're welcome, Crystal, and I'm about to look at the email you sent me."

As Jamila was going over the email that Crystal sent her, she ran across her father's name on some of the indictment papers. As she read them over and over, they weren't making any sense to her, so she called Crystal back.

"Crystal."

"Hey, Jamila, what's up?"

"I was looking over some of these papers you sent me and this name came up on the indictment papers."

"What's the name?" Crystal asked.

"Anthony Catwell."

"Hold on, let me pull him up."

"Okay."

"Hello, Jamila?"

"Yea, I'm still here, Crystal."

"Okay, I remember this case. He was a mob boss and a damn good accountant and very good at his job. He never got caught for murder. Now in this case he was doing some work for Tony Leechee at the time when there was oceanfront view property for sale. Now at the time Felipe and Stone were just making a rising in building their empire. At the time Mr. Catwell was one of the biggest undercover kingpins. He would use stocks and bonds to hide his money from where it was coming from, and Tony Leechee would sell his drugs."

"So, if Mr. Catwell was clean, where did the indictment come from, Crystal?" asked Jamila.

"They NYCPD got a tip on him and all he was doing, and the paper trail went right to him."

"Do you know where the tip came from?"

"Yes, it was Felipe who tipped the police off about him. Now at that time, Jatavious Stone got caught up with twenty kilos of cocaine. Now to set him loose, Felipe agreed to set up Anthony Catwell in a sting. So, for two months they watched him. I also have a file with a bunch of pictures of his wife and little girl."

"Crystal, can you send me them pictures?"

"Sure, hold on, and on 11-12-93 is when they picked him up. There's a video here too. Hold on, I'm playing it now."

"Does the video have sound?"

"Yes."

"Can you send me that video too?"

"Sure. Now they have pictures of Mr. Catwell with Felipe and Stone. Now in the video, he said he knew them from him doing their stocks and bonds. He invested money for them as well. They had him there for hours and he never called a lawyer. Now a newspaper clipping came up, the house burned down, three dead: mother, father, and daughter. Anthony Catwell, age thirty-five. His wife, Jessica Catwell, age thirty and daughter—Jamila Catwell— age eight. Three bodies were found in the house. Wait, wait Jamila, this was your father Anthony Catwell. Oh my God, he faked ya death to protect y'all. Jamila, your father was never found guilty. He was set up, but nothing was able to stick on him."

"Crystal, you are telling me that Felipe and Stone set him up?"

"Yes, it's all in black and white. I sent you everything."

"Thanks, Crystal."

"You're welcome, Jamila."

Within two minutes, Jamila saw over one hundred pictures of her father and mother with her as a little girl. The same video she got from Stone was the same one Crystal just sent her, but this one had sound. It was 12:30 p.m. when Lorenzo called Jamila.

SAYNOMORE

Chapter 44

Three Days Later

"Mr. Stone, the girls are here."

"What girls? I haven't ordered any girls to come up? Stop them at the door and find out who sent them up here." Stone walked over to the phone because it was ringing.

"Hello."

"Mr. Stone, this is management. I hope you like our girls. Compliments of the Branch House Hotel."

"So, you sent the girls up here?"

"Yes, sir, I did."

"Okay, thank you."

"You're welcome, sir."

"You can let them in the hotel and send them up."

Before long, there was a knock on the door. Jatavious went and opened the door, then locked it back once the girls entered the room.

"Ladies, ladies, let's enjoy ourselves, shall we!"

"And you must be Mr. Stone."

"Yes, I am, beautiful. Come sit next to me and show an old dog new tricks."

"I got you, daddy."

"And tell me, what's your name?"

"Candy."

"I like candy."

"Now do you, handsome?"

"Yes, I do."

***

Jamila stopped reading the email when she saw Felipe calling her.

"Hello, Felipe, how are things with you?"

"Good, Jamila."

"I'm glad you're back on your feet, Felipe," replied Jamila.

"I'm glad you're okay. Frankie told me what happened to you, Jamila."

"Yes, I got caught slipping."

"He also told me what you said."

"Yes, in this life we live, Felipe, loved ones and friends die all the time. So, Felipe, when is your next trip up here?"

"I don't know, Jamila."

"Well, Felipe, I look forward to seeing you again."

"Likewise, Jamila. So, did you take care of that little problem for me?" asked Felipe.

"Yes, as we speak, it's getting taken care of. I know it's been a few weeks, but a lot has happened to the both of us."

"I know, Jamila, but that's why I put my trust in you."

"Thank you for trusting me. I'll call you when the deed is done."

"I'll be waiting on your call."

"Take care, Felipe."

Jamila looked at her phone once she hung up. She couldn't believe that she let Jatavious Stone and Felipe get over on her like that. It's been a few weeks, and her face wasn't messed up anymore. Besides, her arm and leg were doing better. She promised herself that both of them were going to die a horrible death. She needed to clear her head. It was 9:40 p.m., so she went to *Passions* to check up on Symone. When she pulled up, like always, the club was jumping. She made her way to the office from the back door, stopping at the bar first to get a bottle of Grey Goose. The DJ saw her, and gave her a shout-out. Jamila threw her hand up to him, and walked up the stairs to Symone's office. Jamila saw two bodyguards at the door.

150

"What's going on in there?" asked Jamila.

"Mrs. LaCross, Symone had us stand out here to make sure no one comes in."

"Okay, ya stand right here and do what she asked."

As Jamila walked through the doors, she saw Symone standing there with a golf club in her hand, with Trap tied on the floor. Symone didn't see Jamila come in, so she stayed by the back door and was watching everything on the other side of the office. Jamila put her finger over her mouth to let the bouncer know to be quiet. She ain't want Symone to know she was there.

"Trap, are you fucking crazy! You shot my sister and tried to kill her. What the fuck was you thinking?" asked Symone.

"It wasn't me, I swear, it was Ace."

"It was you, Trap, and I ain't say fucking talk, nigga."

Symone smacked him in the face with the golf club, making blood and some of his teeth fly out of his mouth.

"Please don't do this, it wasn't me, I swear," explained Trap in pain.

"Fuck nigga, you ain't try to stop them so in my eyes you was a part of that shit." Symone smacked him in the face again. "I ain't going to shoot your punk ass. That would be too easy. My sister went through pain, so you going to feel the same pain, nigga. I can promise you that. You two pull that muthafucker's pants down."

"No, Symone, no, don't do this please, it wasn't me."

"Was you there?"

"Yeah, but I didn't pull the trigger."

"Too fucking bad on your part then because this shit is going to fucking hurt."

Jamila watched as Symone cut his body and poured bleach on his cuts, then she rammed the golf club up his ass. Symone made him feel everything. She just watched as Symone was kicking him in the face over and over again.

"Pussy nigga."

"Symone."

Symone turned around when she heard Jamila's voice.

"I found him, sis, I got his ass."

"I know. I saw everything, where was he at?" asked Jamila.

"Hiding in pink houses."

Jamila looked down at Trap. "Look at you now, Trap, hurt and I think you know you are going to die."

Trap looked up with blood all over his face.

"Red Invee, I'm sorry. I really am."

"I forgive you, Trap, now go sleep in peace." Jamila looked at Symone, and nodded. Symone walked up to her desk, and picked up her gun, then walked back to Trap and placed it to his head, pulling the trigger, blowing his brains out on the floor. Jamila smiled, looking at her lil' sister.

"Symone."

"Yes."

"Next time put plastic down so you won't put blood everywhere."

"You proud of me, sis?"

"I'm always proud of you, beautiful. Hey, y'all can clean up this mess and dump the body somewhere for me. Damian, can you close up for me tonight?"

"Yes, I can, Mrs. LaCross."

"Thank you! Symone, come on let's get you cleaned up."

Once back at Symone's house, she took a shower. Jamila put her clothes in bleach. Once out of the shower, Symone laid her head on Jamila's lap."

"Sis."

"Yes, beautiful."

"I love you!"

"I love you more."

Chapter 45

"Where am I?"

"Good morning, Mr. Jatavious Stone."

"Lorenzo, what the fuck is all of this?"

"It's where you're going to be for a very long time, and this is your past catching up with you."

"How did I get here?"

"One of your party girls drugged you for me."

"Why am I only in my boxers?" asked Stone.

"To make sure you don't have a tracking device on you. I was nice to leave your socks and boxers on you, but don't worry, Jamila will be here in a few hours to answer all the questions you need answering."

"So, I guess this is my final destination?"

"Mr. Stone, let's just say history repeats itself." Lorenzo walked off and called Jamila.

"Hello."

"Hey, we are back."

"Where are y'all at?" asked Jamila.

"The waste plant."

"Okay, I'll be there in an hour."

"Okay, I'll see you in a few."

Jamila placed her phone down on the table.

"Symone, wake up, beautiful, we have something to take care of."

"Where are we going?" asked Symone.

"To my house. Get in your car and follow me."

"Okay."

Jamila watched as Symone followed her to her house.

***

"Fabio, why do you keep flying back and forth to Paris so much?"

Frankie took a deep breath and sat down on a lawn chair in the back yard while talking to Fabio on the phone.

"Frankie, I haven't been all the way honest with you. I have a three-year-old son out there."

"Does Jamila know?" asked Frankie.

"No, I haven't told her yet."

"Fabio, are you still with his mother?"

"Yes and no, Frankie. I love Jamila, but I love my son more."

"So, why you ask her to marry you then?"

"Because I want her in my life. I just don't know what to do."

"Fabio, if Jamila finds out you are sleeping with this lady, it could end very badly for the both of you.

"Frankie, Jamila changed, she has no heart. She's just a stone-cold killer."

"Fabio, we made her that way. We put her in the middle of a war and left her there to make it on her own. We took her here, we are to blame. She has been loyal to us from day one and you owe it to her to be truthful to her."

"I just don't know, Frankie."

"What happened to you, Fabio? You used to be more stand up and hold your ground."

"I want to see my son grow up, Frankie, and that's all that matters. Now I need to take care of something, Frankie, and I have a plane to catch. So, I'll call you when I get to Paris." Fabio hung up the phone and placed it on the dresser. When Jamila pulled up to the house, she saw Fabio packing his car with his suitcase.

"Hey, baby, where you going?"

"I have to make another trip to Paris."

"Fabio, this is the second time this month."

"I know, baby, but you know how business goes."

"I do. Symone, come here, beautiful. Fabio, you remember my sister Symone, right?"

"How can I forget her! Nice to see you again, Symone."

"You too, Fabio."

"Come on, baby, give me a hug, you know I have a plane to catch."

"Fabio, when are you coming back?" asked Jamila.

"In a few weeks, baby."

Jamila watched as Fabio got in his truck and drove off.

"Come on, Symone, let's go inside."

"Damn! Sis, you are living good up in here."

"Thanks, it wasn't easy getting here, I tell you."

"Hey, I think Fabio left his phone here."

"Are you sure?" replied Jamila.

"Is this it?"

"Yeah, let me take it and put it on the kitchen table. He will be back for it." Jamila was about to turn his phone off when a message popped up:

Hey baby, I can't wait to see you too. Have a safe trip, we love you! Tammie.

Jamila read it two more times to make sure she was reading it right. Without saying a word, she walked out of the kitchen to Symone.

"Come on, sis, we have some business to take care of now."

That's when Fabio pulled back up.

"Hey, baby, I left my phone."

"I know. Tammie left you a message on your phone."

Fabio made a move to grab Jamila's arm.

"Please don't touch me. Fabio, when Lorenzo told me it was something funny going on with you, I ain't want to believe it."

"Jamila, I ain't want you to find out this way."

"Fabio, just do both of us a favor and be gone when I get back. Take all ya shit with you, and whatever you leave will be in the trash if you don't take it with you. I don't want no part of you anymore. Here, take this back too, I guess diamonds ain't forever."

Jamila walked out of the house as Fabio just watched her leave. Symone was in the car, waiting for her to come outside.

"Are you okay, sis?" asked Symone.

"Yeah, I am, beautiful."

"So, where are we going?"

"To see one of our father's old friends. We are going to the waste plant."

***

"Jatavious, you ready to talk to Jamila? See you dropped the ball more than once. Jamila is the queen don and you took out a contract on her."

Jatavious looked at Lorenzo with a look of confusion.

"Oh, you ain't think I knew that, huh? Yeah, they came and talked to us about the deal you tried to make and all. Now Red Invee was mad at first because they should have come sooner, but they took themselves out of the hot seat and put you in it."

"I don't know what you're talking about," replied Jatavious.

"Sure you do."

Lorenzo turned his head to see Jamila and Symone walking into the warehouse.

"Jamila, can you tell me the meaning of having me kidnapped and tied to a damn chair?"

"Sure, I can. For years you lied to me on top of putting a contract on me and having my father killed in the worst way. To make a point after you got caught with twenty kilos of cocaine. So, yeah, I have you tied to a chair, Mr. Stone. See, your past came back to haunt you, and it did haunt badly. Now I want my father's blood out of you, but before you die someone wants to speak to you."

Symone looked as Jamila talked, watching every move she made. Jamila pulled out the phone from her bag and called Felipe.

"Hello."

"Felipe, how are you?"

"I'm good. I was just thinking about you."

"Well, I have Jatavious Stone here, hold on let me put you on speaker phone."

"Jatavious, how are you doing, old friend?" asked Felipe.

"So, you had her do your dirty work, Felipe?"

"Just like how you tried to have me killed at the dog track. It's a dog-eat-dog world, Jatavious."

"Felipe, I will see your weak ass in hell, but before you hang up this phone shouldn't Red Invee know that the dog track and the

Oceanfront Property belonged to her father? And before we killed him, he signed everything over to Jamila. I still hear his voice, *Please don't hurt my children*, right before you pulled the trigger blowing his fucking brains out. Yeah, Jamila, Felipe killed your father and raped your mother that night. The man who has you doing his dirty work for him."

That's when the phone went dead. Jamila looked at Symone, then Lorenzo and Masi.

"Masi, go cut the grinder on now. Lorenzo, go get me his pinky ring, and I want it."

Jamila watched as Lorenzo took Stone's pinky ring off.

"Jamila, you can't do this to me, you can't, you hear me!"

"I can do whatever I want to do. I'm the don of the city and you are a dead man."

"Jamila."

"Yes, Symone."

"He had our father killed?"

"Yeah, he did."

"I'm not going to kill him sis, but I do want his blood on my hands too," replied Symone.

Jamila nodded at Symone and stepped to the side, watching as Symone walked up to Jatavious Stone.

"Here you go, Jamila. What is she about to do to him?"

"I don't know, Lorenzo, but she said she wasn't going to kill him."

"So, you killed my father? You took my father away from me before he could hold me!" said Symone.

"Fuck your father, he's dead."

Without saying a word, Symone pulled out her knife and cut Jatavious's beard off. Then she smiled at him, stabbing him in the mouth. His screams rent the air, his legs sticking straight out, shaking as Symone cut his tongue out of his mouth. She picked up his tongue, and walked back to Jamila as he screamed in pain. Masi smacked him in the face, making him dizzy as Lorenzo untied him from the chair. Masi and Lorenzo picked him up, and threw him in the grinder—feet first. Jamila watched everything as he yelled in agony until he was dead.

"Lorenzo, can you clean this place up? Symone, come on, we need to go check something out."

Jamila called Crystal as they were driving off.

"Symone, go to Jelani's."

"Hello, Crystal, I need you to look into something for me ASAP."

"Sure, what is it?"

"There are two properties I want you to see who the owners are. One is Oceanfront and the other is the dog track in South Hampton."

"Sure, I can pull that up now, just give me a second."

Jamila had a beep on the other line. She looked and saw it was Felipe calling her. She said to herself she would call him back once she got off the phone with Crystal to see if Jatavious was telling the truth.

"Hello, Jamila, I'm sorry it took me longer than I was expecting, but both properties have your name on them. You've been the owner for years since you were a little girl."

"Okay, thank you, Crystal. Let me call you back." Jamila saw Felipe was calling her back again.

"Hello, Felipe."

"Jamila, we need to talk."

"You know what, Felipe, I'm done talking to you. You and Jatavious have been feeding me lies, so we have no more business. I did what you asked me to do, so that means our ties are over. I will be taking over all my properties. Other than that, bye, Felipe."

"Jamila, let's not hang up on bad terms," replied Felipe.

Jamila hung up the phone with no more words to say.

"Are you okay, sis?" asked Symone.

"Symone, in this life there will always be problems, after one comes another one. No matter how many rocks you get passed, there will always be three more in front of you waiting." Lorenzo texted Jamila to let her know he got rid of all the firewood they cut up, and cleaned the place up. When they pulled up at Jelani's, Symone parked in the back and went in through the back door.

"Come on, Symone, this is my office."

"Sis, this place is fly as fuck!"

"Thanks, beautiful!"

"Who are these people right here on the wall in this picture with you?" asked Symone.

"My best friends—Elisha, Nayana, Isaiah, and Lorenzo."

"Where are the other three?"

"Isaiah got killed behind Elisha's mess and I killed Nayana and Elisha."

Symone looked at Jamila when she said that.

"Why?"

"They were disloyal to me, so they had to die. I can't take the risk of leaving a disloyal person around me because they can cost you your life. Symone, have a seat. I need to talk to you. Listen, being a part of the mafia is more than just killing people. You killed two people within the last few months you've been around me. I need to be a thinker of all things, Symone."

"I understand, sis."

"Good because in this life you live by the gun, you die by the gun. This is a kill-or-get-killed life. And you need to know just because we are sisters doesn't mean I will treat you differently. So, there is no pass with me."

"I understand, sis," replied Symone.

"Good, so are you sure you want to live this life? Because if you say *yes*, there's no turning back at all."

"I love you, sis, and I want to be just like you and daddy. So, yes, I want to walk in you and our father's footsteps."

"Okay, Symone. There are two rules you must always follow. Never talk to anybody outside of our family about our family business, and always stay loyal to our family and you will have a bright future with us. Now, I have to take care of some business, so you can take my car home and I'll pick it up tomorrow from you."

"I was going to order some food downstairs."

"You can order your food up here if you want," replied Jamila.

"No, I was going to call Slim Boogie to come to eat with me."

"Okay, well, I'll be down there in a little while."

Jamila watched as Symone walked out of her office. Walking to the top of the stairs, Symone looked down at the waterfall and everything else. Symone walked downstairs and smiled to herself, as she sat at a table. *I'm now a part of the LaCross family*, she thought, as she pulled out her phone and called Slim Boogie.

"Hello."

"Hey, Slim, look, I'm at Jelani's and I wanted to know do you want to have dinner with me?"

"Yeah, that sounds good. I'm walking through the park now. I'll be there in twenty minutes."

"Okay, I'll order some food for us so it will be here when you get here."

***

"Lorenzo, this shit is crazy. We have three bags of a chopped-up body. Jamila really doesn't play."

"Badii, if you cross her you die. She doesn't care who you are. She killed our best friend and told me about it a few days later, and I see she likes Masi."

"You can tell?" asked Badii.

"Yeah, I can. She had him drive her to the waste plant with Symone."

"So, what was the point of video recording this nigga getting chopped up?"

"Because he did the same thing to her father, that's why. Now come on, we need to dump his chopped-up body in the Hudson and go see what Jamila has planned for Felipe."

"You think she's going to try and get at him too?"

"Yeah, I do, Badii."

"Lorenzo, Felipe is a Mexican drug lord. This shit going to be a replay of *Scarface*."

"First off, Scarface wasn't Mexican. But, yeah, Felipe got a lot of pull and the manpower. Listen, Badii, anybody can get killed, remember that. Now put these bags in the trunk and I'll be right back."

Badii looked at Lorenzo as he walked off back inside the warehouse.

***

Symone was sitting at the table, looking through her phone, when Slim Boogie and JayGee came walking through the door. The guard stopped them because of the way they were dressed. Symone got up and walked to the door.

"Hey, ya, it's cool. They came to see me. Come on, ya."

The guards stepped to the side to let them pass.

"Yoo, Symone, this place is dope hand down," replied Slim Boogie.

"Facts, Symone, I ain't never been up in here. Red Invee is really a boss queen."

"No, JayGee, she is not a boss queen. She is NYC queen don, get it right."

"My bad, Symone," replied JayGee.

"Now you good, JayGee."

"But for real, Symone, this place is fly."

"Thanks, JayGee, my sister owns it. Come on, our table is over here. Now I only ordered two meals because I ain't know you were coming, so we going to have to order you something."

"Damn! This is how you doing it now, Symone?"

"It's a little something. So Slim, I asked you to come eat with me because I have good news."

"So what's the good news, Symone?" asked Slim.

"I'm now a part of the LaCross family, JayGee and Slim Boogie."

"Now, Symone, you flexing. We know Red Invee is your sister, but you ain't a part of that style."

"Yoo, JayGee, I can go for it, facts."

Jamila walked up behind them, but no one saw her.

"Yeah, JayGee, why would she lie?"

When he turned around, he saw Jamila, and was at a loss for words.

"How are you doing tonight? Do you mind if I have a seat with ya?" asked Jamila.

"It's your place, Jamila."

"Still it's about respect, Slim Boogie. Now, what do y'all see? I want you to look around."

"Everything I want."

"And you can have it, JayGee, but I'm talking about the way you are dressed up in here. I know you ain't know, but now you do, so don't come in here dressed like that again. And Symone, there is a special surprise for you at *Passions*. So I want you to be there at nine p.m."

"Hey, Jamila, can we come?"

"Slim Boogie, I want you there and you can come too, JayGee. It's to honor Symone as a new member of our family."

Jamila's phone went off, and she saw that it was Frankie.

"Will ya excuse me," she said, as she got up from the table.

"Hello, Frankie."

"Jamila, I just got a call from Felipe. Is everything alright because he was very pissed off?"

"Frankie, he lied to me and had my father's blood on his hands. I'm done with him for good."

"Jamila, please be careful with him."

"I will, but Frankie, let me call you back. I'm having dinner with my sister and her friends."

"No, we will talk tomorrow, Jamila."

"Okay, Frankie, goodbye."

Jamila hung up the phone, and walked back to the table.

Chapter 46

After having dinner with Symone and her friends, Jamila went home. She had so much on her chest, so she took a hot bath and went to sleep. When she woke up, it was 10 a.m. She went downstairs to find a letter from Fabio. At first, she was thinking about throwing it away, but she read it.

Jamila, I really don't know the right words to say. I am truly sorry about all of this. I just hope that you can forgive me one day. You are the only female that I ever loved the way I do. It pains me to know I had a baby with another female and not you. I do regret that night, but now my son...I will never forget the night we met or the loving memories that we shared. It's been nights when you weren't around me and I would just look at your pictures, knowing one day my secret would have to come to the light. I'm lost for words as I write this letter. Just know I will forever love you.

Very truly yours
Fabio

Jamila looked at the letter and shook her head, then she put her engagement ring on it as a paper weight. She had a lot to handle this morning, but instead of driving one of her cars, she put a jogging suit on with a baseball cap and ran ten miles. Something she hadn't done in a while. She made it downtown and decided to go see Nayana and Elisha's grave site. She sat down there for two hours. It was 4 p.m. when she left. She waved down a cab, and went to Symone's house. She still had a few outfits in the other bedroom she never wore.

It was 7 p.m. when she got there. Frankie, Lorenzo, Badii, Muscle, Masi, and seven other members of the LaCross family were sitting at the table when she walked in. She told Symone to be there by 9 p.m.

"Thank you all for coming here tonight. This means a lot to me. Our guests will be here in a little while, then I will tell y'all why I asked y'all to come here tonight."

It was 8:35 p.m. when Symone walked in with Slim Boogie and JayGee with all eyes on them.

"Everyone, this is Symone, Slim Boogie, and JayGee, but tonight is about y'all. From day one Lorenzo and Frankie have been here with me. We lost a lot of members, but we never fell back. Badii, I remember when I asked you to take care of something for me and you did it no questions asked. You've been loyal ever since. Muscle, Masi, y'all did something for me words can't express. So Muscle, Masi, and Badii these are for you."

Jamila handed them all the car keys to 2001 BMWs.

"And one more thing." She gave them all red ruby rings. "You all are Lt's in this family. Lorenzo and I will go over all y'all new positions tomorrow."

Everyone started clapping.

"I have one more announcement to make. We also have one new member here tonight, my little sister—Symone. She is now a part of the LaCross family. About a little over a month ago someone tried to kill me. Within two weeks two of them were dead and one was missing. Symone found him and let's just say at the time death didn't come fast and easy for him. So, for taking care of that, Symone, you showed loyalty to me and this family. Myself and everyone here accept you as one of us, and we welcome you to our family. And because you took it upon yourself to handle that problem, I gave you a green emerald ring. You are now Sgt. In our family."

Everyone stood and clapped for Symone.

"Everyone, please enjoy yourself tonight!"

Jamila felt good looking at her sister, her friends and family all in one place.

"Jamila, can I talk to you for a minute?"

"What's up, Frankie?"

"What's the problem with you and Felipe?" asked Frankie.

"He lied. I found out everything. How he killed my father and stole his property, why?"

"He called me and was very upset."

"So, what's that got to do with me?"

164

"Just watch out is all I'm saying."

"Okay, I will."

***

"Yo, Symone, congratulations, ma!" Slim Boogie said.

"Thank you!"

"Well done, ma."

"Symone, can I talk to you for a minute?" asked Jamila.

"I'll be right back, Slim Boogie. What's up, sis?"

"So, now you are a part of the LaCross family. Symone, I want the best for you at all times and remember the two rules of the family."

"I will."

"I been looking at Slim Boogie. I know he ain't mean to let go of Ace's arm, plus I like him. So, I might let him come to the family. What do you think about that?" asked Jamila.

"I'll talk to him and see if he wants to be a part of the family. Do you want me to call him over here?" asked Symone.

"No, I'm still thinking about it. I'll let you know, but tonight it's all about you, so enjoy your night and we'll talk about this later."

Lorenzo walked up to Jamila.

"Symone, let me go talk to Lorenzo and I'll catch up to you later."

"Okay, sis."

"How she feel about being a part of the family?" asked Lorenzo.

Jamila looked at Symone, then said, "I don't think it hit yet Lorenzo. It's crazy we have a family that is ready for anything that comes our way. We survived two wars, we're not loud and we made it this far and it all started over a murder eight years ago. Lorenzo, we came so far and Crystal helped us along the way."

"You're right, she did."

"You know, Lorenzo, I was thinking about all the people we killed over the three years. We have to move better before we end up dead one day too."

"I know, Jamila, but why you saying this?" asked Lorenzo.

"Because Frankie told me that Felipe is upset, and it crossed my mind. I'm not going to act like I have the manpower to get him killed in his own country. And I really don't know his limits. I'm not going to fool myself, Lorenzo."

"And you don't need to. Now come on, let's enjoy our night. We're here to celebrate the family."

"You're right, we are," replied Jamila.

After a pause, Jamila spoke again. "But Lorenzo, remind me to call Carlos—one of Frankie's friends. He gave me his card before I went to see Felipe last time."

"Okay and just to let you know, Jamila, before I came here, I stopped by your office and put a surprise on your desk."

"Okay, Lorenzo, thank you!" Jamila kissed Lorenzo on the cheek before walking off.

It was 3 a.m. when Jamila made it home. She had two cars follow her, just in case something happened like before. When she walked into her house, there was a box on the table. She pulled her gun out and walked around her house, but no one was there. She walked to the table and opened the box, and there was a rope in it. She knew that was a message that said to hang yourself. She picked up the box, walked back to her car, and left. She knew what Felipe was telling her, he'd made it very clear. Once she got to her other brownstone, she placed the box down on the table, pulled Carlos's number and placed it next to the box so she'll know to call him in the morning.

Chapter 47

Frankie walked outside to his car with one of his guards.

"You see him, Mr. Landon?

"Yeah, I do. Let's see what this pig wants," replied Frankie.

As they walked to the car, Detective Boatman walked up to them.

"Mr. Frankie Landon, how you doing this morning?" said Detective Boatman, smoking his *Black & Mild.*

"Detective, what can I do for you?"

"Since I can't get a good morning, let's cut to the chase. I haven't seen my good friend Fabio in a while. I'm trying to reach him."

"Detective, that's both of us, so when you do find him let me know. I need to talk to him. Now if you would excuse me, I have to be on my way."

As Frankie was about walk past him, Detective Boatman stepped in his path.

"Let me tell you something, old man. You ain't who you used to be and I know that Jamila killed Ace and his little crew. And I also know that you have been backing her up from the beginning. So, when I do decide to take her ass down, just know your ass is going to be on that same fucking bus."

"I don't know who the fuck you think you are, Detective, but let me tell you, something. I know about you from the first meeting you had with Fabio in the alley. But let me tell you this, if you ever come and threaten me again I will pay a visit to your son and mother at 231 Northside Fr. Then I might go see your brother and his family and have them all swimming with the fishes. Now play pussy and get fucked, Boatman."

Frankie looked at him in his eyes without saying a word. Detective Boatman threw his *Black &Mild* down, and walked off.

"Do you want me to take care of him, boss?"

"No, I don't, he gets the picture very clear now and his nigga ass will be swimming with the fishes if he fucks with me one more time.

***

Jamila woke up and picked up the box with the rope inside. She placed it down and called Carlos. It was a deep accent she heard when he answered the phone.

"Hello."

"May I speak to Carlos?" asked Jamila.

"May I ask who is calling?"

"This is Jamila LaCross."

"Yes, this is Frankie's friend. I've been waiting to hear from you. What can I do for you?"

"I was hoping we can talk face to face?" asked Jamila.

"So, are you trying to fly down here?"

"To be honest with you I don't feel comfortable coming down there right now. I was hoping you could come up here."

"I see, I think I can arrange that. Let me give you a call back a little later today. Can I reach you at this number?"

"Yes, this is my direct line."

"Okay, I will call you back then."

"I'll be waiting to hear from you."

After hanging up with Carlos, Jamila called Frankie and told him they needed to talk and to meet her at Jelani's in thirty minutes. Jamila got to Jelani's in ten minutes with the box, and went right to her office. She walked over to her desk, and noticed there was a CD wrapped up. When she put it in the CD player, it was Jatavious Stone going into the grinder feet first. Jamila smiled, knowing that Lorenzo did that for her. Stone was begging for his life as he'd made her father beg for his in torture. Frankie walked into her office, and sat down at her desk. Jamila took the CD out, and put it in the desk drawer.

"Jamila, what was so important that I had to be down here in thirty minutes?" asked Frankie.

"Your friend, Felipe, sent me a gift."

"What?"

She showed him the rope.

"Jamila, he's telling you he's going to let you hang yourself. Now if it had a black person with the rope around the neck that wouldn't be a sign to go kill yourself. Where was the rope at?" asked Frankie.

"In my house."

"Was there anyone else there?"

"No, there wasn't."

"Just walk away, Jamila."

"No, Frankie, I'm not. You gave me Carlos's number and told him about me, why?"

"Carlos has a few contacts and could help you out if needed. So what you plan on doing?" asked Frankie.

"I don't know yet."

"One more question. How you know Felipe sent you this rope and not Jatavious Stone? Or even the man that tried to kill you a few weeks back?"

"Because he's dead and his lil' crew."

"Okay, I give you that. Jamila, walk with me to the window. What do you see?" asked Frankie.

"The city of New York."

"Do you see how big the city is?"

"Yeah."

"Okay, now look at your restaurant. How big is it?"

"I don't know, Frankie."

"Let's just say a few thousand square feet."

"Okay, what's your point?" asked Jamila.

"The point is, Jamila, you represent your restaurant, and Jatavious represents the city of New York. You playing in a whole new ball game now."

"You know what, Frankie? Everyone always underestimates the underdog too, but they are the last ones standing."

"Jamila, I never underestimated you because I know what you could do. I saw it first-hand, I just want you to make sure your family is ready for this game."

"Frankie, do you care to watch a movie with me, well not a movie but just a video clip?"

"What is it?"

"Walk with me back to my desk."

When Jamila showed Frankie the video of Jatavious Stone, he watched while Jamila walked over to the bar and got two glasses. She got a bottle of gin and poured two shots for both of them. She sat down on her desk and crossed her legs as Frankie watched the video clip. He looked up at her.

"When?"

"Yesterday evening!" Jamila took the CD out, closed the laptop, and took her shot. Frankie took his shot and said, "Jamila, that was the first game. Just remember there are several games to win a championship."

Frankie kissed Jamila on the cheek and walked out. Jamila walked to the balcony, and watched him as he left. She had a lot to do and not much time to do it.

Chapter 48

Detective Boatman walked into his office and had a message on his desk from Chief Tafem that said, "Come to my office as soon as you get this message." *What the fuck do you want now?* Boatman thought. Turning around with the cup of coffee he had in his hand, he walked to the chief's office, not knowing what to expect. Detective Boatman knocked two times before opening the door.

"Hey, chief, you wanted to see me?"

Without even looking up, the chief said, "Yes, come in and have a seat."

Closing the door behind him, Detective Boatman took a seat in front of Chief Tafem's door.

"What's that file you're looking over?" asked Boatman.

"Jatavious Stone's file."

Looking up at Detective Boatman, Chief Tafem took his glasses off and placed them on his desk.

"We have a problem here."

"Is that why you are looking over the file?"

"Yes, it is. Rumor has it that Jatavious Stone has been kidnapped from a Las Vegas hotel. Now we don't know for sure, but I did see a video of some party girls going in there and a few hours later they left. Now the girls had painted faces and masks on so we can't make out the faces. Now when they left, four men are seen walking in the room and we couldn't see their faces at all. They weren't in there three minutes prior, and next you see them and Jatavious Stone leaving."

"Was he putting up a fight?"

"No, he wasn't. You could tell he was drugged by the way he was walking."

"Okay, I don't get it that this happened in Las Vegas. Why did you call me to your office about this?"

"Because he works and cleans up our bullshit. And if it happened in Las Vegas, that means some fucking how it's connected from Queens. So, I need you to do what you do and talk to the people who want to talk to me. You know your underground friends who won't to talk to nobody at this department."

"So, I guess this is my case now too?" asked Boatman.

"No, it's not. I'm just asking for a favor. Stone owed some very important people a lot of money and he's been missing for seventy-two hours. Now no one can find him and yesterday this tape popped up on my desk. So now I'm asking for help."

"I'll see what I can do, Chief."

"Boatman, I need to know something by tonight, no later than 11 o'clock tomorrow morning. So, I'm asking you to pull out all your aces in the deck of cards on this one."

"Chief, I'll go talk to a few people, but you know how they play, so watch out because I'mma let them know you are the one who is asking," replied Boatman.

"I'm just giving you a heads up."

"I understand."

When Detective Boatman walked out of Chief Tafem's office, it was like everyone was looking at him. He went to his office, got his coat off the back of his chair, and walked out of the police station to his car.

***

"Oso, when was the last time you saw Red Invee?" asked Morwell

"It's been a few months now," Oso replied.

"I had a feeling you was going to say that. My contacts are telling me she's been doing a lot of business with Felipe and if that's the case she's breaking her contract with us."

Oso looked at Morwell smoking his cigar with his legs crossed in an all-white suit, drinking his brandy outside on the deck of his house.

"Brother, I haven't seen her, but her payments for her orders are still coming in. She is still shopping with us, that has not changed."

172

"I want you and LK to go pay her a visit and see if these rumors true. And if so, hear what she has to say and if it don't add up, kill her. No, bring her back here for me to kill her myself."

"I'm on my way to go see her now, Brother."

***

"What do I owe the pleasure of New York's finest?" Joe Scott took a pause from the pool game he was playing. He laid down his pool stick and picked up the 8 ball. "You know, detective, you just fucked up an eight hundred dollar pool game."

"We need to talk."

"What is it you want to talk about?"

Detective Boatman looked around at everyone looking at him.

"I need to find Jatavious Stone. You know where he's at?"

"You come in my place of business and stop my pool game to ask me about a nigga? Let me tell you something, Detective Boatman, I pay you to keep the police off my ass and to handle my dirty work. I don't pay you to come to ask me questions about a nigga."

"You are using that N-word a little too much right now," Detective Boatman said, looking into his face.

"Well, let me say this, Detective Boatman, I don't know shit about no murder, is that clear enough for you?"

"Like water, but since I'm here let me get that fifteen thousand dollars. It's payment day today. Your bill is due. "

"Rocky, pay the man minus the eight hundred dollars he made me lose. Detective, if you don't mind, I have a game to play. I'm sure you can see your way out."

He watched Detective Boatman leave out the door.

"Rocky, I'll catch up on this game right now—I have a phone call to make—You know out of all the niggas in NYC, I hate that one the most," Joe said as he walked to the back office.

***

Jamila walked into her office and before she could sit down, her office phone went off.

"Hello."

"Mrs. LaCross, you have a Detective Boatman down here to see you."

"Do you mind bringing him up to my office please?"

"No, Mrs. LaCross, we are on the way now."

Jamila checked her gun, and placed it in her desk drawer. That's when she heard a knock at the door.

"Come in. Detective Boatman, please come in and have a seat. Thank you for bringing him up, Kim, that will be all."

Jamila walked to her bar, and got two glasses and a bottle of Cîroc, then placed them on her desk as she took her seat.

"So, tell me, Detective Boatman, what do I owe the pleasure of this visit?"

Detective Boatman picked up the bottle of Cîroc, and poured himself and Jamila two shots.

"To get to the point, I'm looking for Jatavious Stone. Now you don't have to help me find him, but I will tell you this. There is going to be a lot of heat coming down if I don't get some answers soon."

"So, is that a threat, Detective?" replied Jamila.

"No, it's a promise, but I'm not the one who is going to come after you or everybody else. It's Chief Tafem who is the one that needs to know the truth behind his missing. I don't give two fucks about him. I'm only coming to you because you are the queen don. So, who you think they are going to look at first?" asked Detective Boatman.

"Detective, you need to walk very light with me. Now I don't care how much heat comes down on Chief Tafem's head but know this, Detective—Just like you have pictures of me doing what I do, I have videos of you doing what you do. So, let me show you something."

Detective Boatman looked at Jamila with hate in his eyes as she pulled out her laptop and pressed play for him. He sat there watching the video of him killing in the alley a few months back.

"See, Detective, the look on your face is priceless. I had my P.I. follow you for me and that's what he came back to me with. So, from this point on, your payments are over from me. And next time you think about coming to threaten me, think twice because now the rabbit has the gun. This is what I will do. I'll go see Chief Tafem to see what he has to say tonight. So, take your shot, Detective, and see your way out."

Detective Boatman took his shot, placed his glass on the desk, and walked out of Jamila's office. Jamila just looked at him, knowing she couldn't wait to stand over his dead fucking body. She picked up the phone and called Lorenzo.

"Hey, Lorenzo, I need you, Masi, and Badii to come with me somewhere tonight."

"Sure, what time and where?" asked Lorenzo.

"In a few hours just be on standby," replied Jamila.

"Just call me, I'll be waiting."

Jamila was about getting up when her phone went off.

"Hello."

"Good morning, Mrs. LaCross, it's Carlos."

"Hey, Carlos."

"Did I catch you at a bad time?"

"No, you didn't," replied Jamila.

"Okay. I'm sending someone to come talk to you for me. They will be up there this week."

"Okay, what is his or her name?" asked Jamila.

"It will be my business partner—Lopez. I will call you when he is on the way to you."

"Okay, I will be waiting to hear from you."

"I'll be in touch, Mrs. LaCross."

After hanging up the phone, Jamila took her shot and walked to her bird cage, knowing what she had to do tonight.

***

Detective Boatman walked back to the police station and walked to his office. He saw Chief Tafem and winked at him. He nodded back at Boatman and went into his office. Chief Tafem couldn't help but think about what Detective Boatman did or who he talked to, but what he did know was that he will have some answers soon and he can get a lot of muthafuckers off his ass.

***

It was 9 o'clock that night when Badii knocked on Chief Tafem's door. Jamila was parked in front of his house in a limo when he came to the door.

"Chief Tafem, someone wants to talk to you."

Chief Tafem looked at Badii, Masi, and Lorenzo standing next to the limo.

"Who wants to talk to me?" asked Chief Tafem.

"I think you know already. Are you coming or not?"

Chief Tafem closed his eyes for a second, then walked out the front door, and closed the door behind him. Jamila watched as Badii walked him to the limo. Masi patted him down, then Lorenzo opened the door for him to get in and closed it once he got in. Chief Tafem looked at Jamila. She was outstanding and beautiful; he couldn't take his eyes off of her.

"Hello, Chief Tafem. I hope me coming by I ain't interrupt anything?"

"No, I was just going to heat some food up then lay down, that's all," replied Chief Tafem.

"At least you weren't waiting in my house this time."

"Again I apologize about that. So, tell me, how can I help you?"

"Detective Boatman said you needed to talk to me."

"Mrs. LaCross, I don't want no problems. I'm just trying to find out what happened to Jatavious Stone. He owes a lot of money out to a lot of very important people.

"So, what does this got to do with you? Matter of fact, hold that thought for one second please," replied Jamila. She tapped the window two times; that's when Lorenzo opened up the door.

"Yes, Mrs. LaCross?"

"Follow us."

"Yes, Mrs. LaCross."

Jamila told the limo driver to go to the waste plant.

"Chief Tafem, I would like you to take a ride with me, if you don't mind. Now tell what you were saying?"

The look in Chief Tafem's eyes while taking a deep breath questioned whether he was going to die.

"Mrs. LaCross, Jatavious Stone had a deal which he was going to give someone Oceanfront Property for the debt he owed, but he's been missing for seventy-two hours now. All we know is that he was drugged and carried out of a hotel in Las Vegas."

"So, again what does his absence have to do with you?" replied Jamila.

"Because whoever took him we know the call came from here."

"Ummm, I understand, Chief Tafem."

When they pulled up to the waste plant, the limo stopped, and the door opened.

"After you, Chief Tafem."

"Where are we?" asked Chief Tafem.

"Somewhere we can talk at, just the two of us, Chief Tafem."

As they walked into the building, Chief Tafem looked at Badii, Lorenzo, and Masi, wondering if they were going to kill him. Nobody said a word when the warehouse doors opened to reveal boxes and barrels everywhere. It was pitch-black in there.

"Watch your step and follow my voice, Chief Tafem."

That's when Jamila opened the door to her office.

"Please come in and have a seat. Masi, you can wait on the outside of the door, you and Badii. So, tell me, Chief Tafem, how can Jatavious Stone give someone two properties away that don't belong to him?"

"What you mean not his?"

"See, the properties belong to me." Jamila opened up her desk drawer and pulled out a file and handed it to him. "So, let me ask you this again. Who does Mr. Stone owe money to?"

Chief Tafem looked at Lorenzo, then Jamila.

"Mrs. LaCross, please don't take this the wrong way, but I can't tell you. I'm not supposed to tell anyone this, so don't take it as disrespect."

"I'm not. I promise you that, Chief Tafem. Do you care for a drink?" asked Jamila.

"No, thank you."

"Let me show you something, Chief Tafem." Jamila pulled out her laptop as Chief Tafem handed her back the files. She turned the screen around so he could see the video of Jatavious Stone being cut into pieces. Chief Tafem's face turned pale white as he watched Jatavious Stone yelling and screaming as he went into the grinder feet first. He put his hands over his mouth so he didn't throw up.

"Chief Tafem, not in my office and not on my floor. Chief, I need you to look at me. You have a five-year-old daughter and a seven-year-old son. Your mother lives in Freeport, Long Island on Matterson Ave. Apt. 321B, and your wife works at parenthood. I'm telling you this because if I hear one word about this video, I will make you watch as this happens to your family. Do I make myself clear?"

Chief Tafem nodded.

"So Chief Tafem, how much money does Jatavious Stone give and to who?" asked Jamila.

Chief Tafem was shaking out of control; that's when Jamila knew she had him.

"To the Temple. It's seven of them and he owes them."

"Mr. Red, I would like names please."

"I swear I don't know no names. The only name I know is Jordan Mark. May I please have that drink now?"

"Sure, Lorenzo, can you please get Chief Tafem a drink? So, how much does he owe them? Lorenzo, can you please go count out two point five million dollars for me?"

178

"Sure, I'll be back in thirty minutes," replied Lorenzo.

"Oh and put an extra one million dollars to the side."

"Okay, Mrs. LaCross!"

"Chief Tafem, thank you for taking the time out to talk to me tonight."

"Mrs. LaCross, may I ask you a question?" asked Chief Tafem.

"Yes, you may."

"Why me when you could have just talked to Detective Boatman?"

"I never talked to Detective Boatman, we just have a mutual friend. Plus, I wanted to talk to you face to face. Would you care for another drink?"

"Yes, please. Do you mind if I smoke in here?"

"No, go right ahead."

Lorenzo walked into the office a few minutes afterwards with two bags in his hands, and placed them on Jamila's desk.

"Thank you, Lorenzo!"

"No problem."

"Chief Tafem, in this bag there is two point five million dollars and in this bag, there is one million dollars. My question to you is, would you like to work for me?"

"What would I have to do?"

"We will talk about that later. Right now, just make sure the Temple gets this money and you take the one million dollars for yourself. I will be in touch. Lorenzo will take you back to the limo and my driver will drop you off home. Thank you for taking the time out to talk to me tonight, Chief Tafem. Lorenzo, can you take him to the limo?"

"Sure. Right this way, Chief Tafem."

Picking up the two bags, Chief Tafem followed Lorenzo out of Jamila's office.

SAYNOMORE

Chapter 49

Detective Boatman walked into his office and had a message from Chief Tafem. He walked to Chief Tafem's office. Chief Tafem was in there drinking his cup of coffee, and smoking a cigar when he opened the door.

"Good morning, Chief!"

"Close the door, detective, sit down."

"Chief, are you okay?" asked Boatman.

"Shit! I don't know where to start. She came to see me last night, her and her goons. That woman is the fucking devil."

"What did she say?"

"I don't want to talk about it. She gave me one million dollars and two point five million to give to the Temple."

"So Chief, you told her about the Temple?"

Taking a long drag of his cigar, he looked at Detective Boatman.

"Yeah, I had no fucking choice."

"Sir, what did she do to you last night?" asked Boatman.

"Nothing, I need you to take a ride with me."

"No problem, sir."

***

Detective Boatman looked at Chief Tafem the whole time. He was driving, shaking, and smoking back to back, not saying a word. When they pulled up to the grand capital, Chief Tafem grabbed the bags with the money and stepped out of the car.

"Boatman, let's get this shit over with."

"Sir, you sure you are okay to do this?" asked Boatman.

"I just need to get this shit done now, right now."

There were seven people looking at Chief Tafem and Detective Boatman when they walked in the room. A voice came from the back of the table.

"Chief Tafem, now tell us what was so urgent you had to meet us today? Please tell us."

"I have the two point five million that Jatavious Stone owes the Temple."

"So, you talked to him is what you are telling us?"

"No, I have not," replied Chief Tafem.

"So, how do you have the money he owes then? How did you get it then?"

"I had a visitor last night who came and dropped the money off to me."

They all looked around the table at each other.

"Where is Jatavious Stone at, Chief Tafem?"

"I don't know."

"So, who gave you this money?"

"With the most respect, can you just take the money?"

"No, it's not about the money, Chief Tafem. It never was. We need the Oceanfront Property. Now who gave you the money?"

"Jamila LaCross gave me the money and Jatavious Stone never owned the properties. It has always been hers."

"Not true, that is a false statement."

"No, sir, it's not."

"Chief Tafem, do you know something that we don't?"

"Jamila LaCross's father was Anthony Catwell and before he died, he signed all his property over to her and Oceanfront was one of them."

"Are you telling me that Anthony Catwell was Jamila La-Cross's father?"

"Yes, sir, I am and she is willing to pay what Jatavious owed the Temple."

"Why is she willing to do that? Matter of fact, is there any way you can set up a meeting for us with her?"

"I can see what I can do sir."

"Chief Tafem, take the money back to her and we expect to hear from her very soon."

Chief Tafem picked up the bag, then he and Detective Boatman walked out the room.

"What now, Chief?" asked Boatman.

"We get back in touch with Mrs. LaCross and give her the money back and tell her they want a meeting with her."

SAYNOMORE

Chapter 50

It was 3:45 p.m. that afternoon when Jamila's limo pulled up at Jelani's. Masi and Badii were outside waiting on her to pull up. When the limo stopped, Masi walked over to her door and opened it for her.

"Good afternoon, Mrs. LaCross."

"Good afternoon, Masi."

That's when Badii walked over to her.

"Mrs. LaCross, you have a guest inside waiting on you."

Masi was looking around outside as Badii was talking to Jamila.

"And who is this guest inside waiting on me?"

"Detective Boatman, he's at the bar."

"Okay, stay by my side while Badii leads Detective Boatman to my office."

"Yes, Mrs. LaCross."

Jamila was so concerned about why Detective Boatman was there. She didn't see Crystal and her co workers sitting at the table she passed on the way to her office.

"Masi, I want you to stand on the outside of this door when Detective Boatman comes in here, and don't move until he leaves. Do I make myself clear?"

"Yes, you do, Mrs. LaCross," replied Masi.

"Good." Jamila opened up her office door and went inside. Badii walked Detective Boatman to her office door, and knocked twice before opening the door. Detective Boatman walked in with the brown bag in his hand. Badii nodded at Jamila, and she nodded, letting him know he could leave.

"So, Detective Boatman, have a seat and tell me what I can do for you today," said Jamila.

"I came to return this two point five million you gave to Chief Tafem."

Jamila looked at the bag in his hand.

"So tell me, detective, why did you come and not Chief Tafem?"

"You shook him up last night. The man almost pissed himself. I also have a message for you from the Temple."

Jamila locked her fingers together as she leaned on her desk.

"So, tell me this message you have for me."

"The members from the Temple want to have a meeting with you."

"They do?"

"You know what, Red Invee? You think you're just too smart. I'll give you this, you have the first black mafia family in NYC. You made your rise to the top and became the first black female don, but let me say this mafia don't hold a candle to the flame that the Temple holds. So, you might want to see what they have to say."

"Detective Boatman, you are right, but you see the difference between me and them is that I'm going where they ain't going to go and that's why I'm the queen don. I will go have this meeting with the Temple, let's say Friday around three p.m. Is that good?" Red Invee smiled.

"I'll let them know."

Jamila watched as Detective Boatman got up and walked out her office. Once he closed the door, she got up and picked up the bag with the money inside and walked to her hidden office, where she placed the bag in the safe before walking out. When she opened up the office door, Masi was still there waiting on her.

"Masi, walk with me downstairs. I honestly hate that man, Masi."

"Do you want me to take care of him for you, Mrs. LaCross?"

"No, I can't touch him right now. He has so much on our family that his death could be the end of the LaCross family if it ever gets out, so we just have to play it smart right now. I promise you this—his day is coming and I hope it is a very painful day."

As Jamila was walking through the restaurant, Crystal called her name out. Masi stopped and looked at them.

"It's okay, Masi, I will catch up with you later. Just keep an eye out on my floor."

"Hello, beautiful, how are you and your co-workers enjoying the meal?"

"It's to die for. We are loving it, Mrs. LaCross!"

"I'm glad you are." Jamila saw a waiter, and snapped her fingers at him to come to the table.

"Yes, Mrs. LaCross?"

"Bring two bottles of champagne to this table on ice right now."

"Yes, Mrs. LaCross."

"Crystal, I have to run, but whatever you need just let me know, beautiful."

"There is one thing, can we take a picture with you if you don't mind?" asked Crystal.

"Sure, come on!"

Oso watched as Jamila took her pictures with her guests from the corner table of the restaurant. He watched as Jamila smiled and kissed Crystal on the cheek before she walked off. Jamila listened as she sauntered off, leaving the company to Crystal and her friends.

"Crystal, you did not tell us you knew Jamila LaCross. She is the don of NYC. I can't believe you are her friend."

Jamila just smiled as she heard them talk to each other about her. She saw one of Oso's men leaving the bathroom. She stopped and looked at him. That's when she saw Oso sitting at a table, eating with two more of his men. She walked over to the table where he was at.

"Hello, Oso, why you ain't tell me you were coming up?"

"I thought it would be best this way. Please have a seat with me."

"Sure, so what brings you up here?"

Before Oso said a word, his two men stood up from the table and turned their backs to them. Masi and Badii saw them and walked over there with Jamila, and stood right in front of Oso's men. Jamila put her hand up to tell them to stay there.

"Jamila, word got back to Morwell that you were buying your contents from Felipe, is that true?" asked Oso.

"Yes, it is, Oso, but it's more to the story than just me buying contents from Felipe."

"Do you mind sharing with me then so I can have a clear understanding of this relationship you and Felipe have?"

"Oso, out of respect for you and your brother and all the help you gave me along the way, I do not mind. Twenty years ago, Felipe and Jatavious Stone killed my father. I just found this out a few months back. So, I got close enough to them and I avenged my father's death. I already took care of Jatavious Stone, now I'm going after Felipe and I was buying from them to make it look like a business relationship until I found out what I needed to know. Now, I know the truth and as of last week I cut Felipe off."

"So, are you telling me you have no more dealing with him?" asked Morwell.

"The next time Felipe sees me I will be standing over his body with my gun pointed at his head."

"That's all I needed to hear, then I will let Morwell know what you said. Remember, Jamila, in this line of work, loyalty is everything."

"Oso, if I would have told you that I was choosing to deal with him, how would this meeting have turned out?" asked Jamila.

Oso put a piece of steak in his mouth, then pointed at the window. When Jamila looked, there was a man standing with a .30-30 Winchester pointed at her from across the street in the park next to the bushes. She looked at Oso.

"Jamila, it's just business." He put his fork down, wiped his mouth, and got up from the table. He walked around where Jamila was at, and kissed her cheek. Jamila didn't say a word as Oso walked off.

"Mrs. LaCross, are you good?"

"Yes, Badii, I am. Walk me back to my office. Masi, have my car pulled out front and I'll be down to get it in a few minutes."

After getting her bag and gun out her office, Jamila walked outside to her car.

"Masi, you and Badii stay here until Lorenzo gets here. I'll be back later."

"Are you sure you going to be okay?"

"I'll be fine, Badii."

Jamila found herself driving around NYC for hours. She pulled up at her mother's house and saw her standing at the front door. When she stepped out of the car, the look on her face was shocking and surprising to see Jamila after all these years. Jamila walked up to her without saying a word. As tears came from her mother's eyes, Jamila hugged her.

"I missed you so much, Jamila."

"I missed you too, mom."

"Come inside so we can talk."

Jamila sat down at the table and looked around.

"So where is Victorious at or Mr. Walker?" asked Jamila.

"They are gone for the day."

"So, why you never told me you got remarried or had another child? You ain't even let me know about Symone."

"I was mad at you, Jamila. You were doing so good in school. I just knew you were going to be successful."

"But mommy, I'm very successful. I have over ten businesses and I'm a millionaire."

"But you are living the same life as your father. When he got killed, it took a big part of me and I couldn't take another death like that. So, yes, I distanced myself from you. Just in case something happened to you, it wouldn't hurt so bad."

"I promise, mommy, I'm going to be okay."

"Jamila, you can't promise me that. I saw your car being pulled out of the Hudson River. I dropped to my knees and prayed that you were okay. I emailed you three times and you never replied. What was I supposed to think?"

Jamila lowered her head and knew what her mother was saying was right.

"Mom, I love you and I'm sorry for living the life I live, but can I move you and your family to a better neighborhood, somewhere far from here?" asked Jamila.

"Is something going on I don't know about, Jamila?"

"No, mom, I just want the best for you, that's all."

"So, where you want to move me to?"

"I was thinking Long Island."

"You know what, baby? I've been living in this house for years and I think it's about time to move. So, okay, it's time I moved on with my life."

Jamila stayed to talk with her mother a few more hours before leaving.

Chapter 51

"Frankie, it's good to see you, so how have you been?"

"I've been good, Felipe. The question is, how have you been since your near-death encounter?"

"I haven't been the same, but I will say I been sleeping a lot better since Jatavious Stone's been dead. So, what brings you all the way down here to see me today?" asked Felipe.

"Felipe, we've been friends for a very long time. Today I came to talk to you about Jamila."

"Frankie, are you siding with her?"

"Felipe, she got your gift you sent her."

"And what gift is this?"

"The rope in her house."

"Oh, that gift!" replied Felipe as he smiled.

"Felipe, I need you to hear what I'm about to say."

"I'm listening, Frankie."

"Are you trying to go to war with her?"

"No, Frankie, I'm just letting her know *don't hang yourself*. Come on, walk with me by the water, it's a beautiful day."

"Felipe, I know you are a very powerful man, but Jamila is very good at what she does."

"Frankie, have you heard the saying good is the enemy of greatness? You are right she is good, but I'm great at what I do."

"Felipe, we've been friends for over twenty years and I hope we don't have a falling-out."

"And why would we have a falling-out?"

"Because Jamila is like my child and I will back her against you. So, I'm asking you to let whatever you have against her go for our sake. Jamila is very smart and she is going to reply to the gift you sent her. I took her under my wing, Felipe."

"Don't worry about Jamila, Frankie. Now let's go have a bite to eat and play a round of golf."

"I haven't played golf in years, Felipe."

"That makes two of us. Frankie, you know why I like coming to this river?"

"No, why?"

"Not only can you catch the most beautiful fish, but it goes out for miles and miles. See, you came down here to ask me about Jamila. Thus, not only did you break the rules, but you threatened me by saying you will back her up against me. You are the head of the Landon family. She is the queen don of the LaCross family, and families don't get involved in family wars at all. You think I care that you took that nigga under your wing? Well, I don't give two fucks that you did it at all. So, I'll give her another message to respond to. Just to make sure she gets the message."

Frankie looked to his right, and saw the gun pointed at his head, then he looked back at Felipe.

"Don't worry, I'll see you real soon, motherfucker," replied Frankie.

"Maybe you will, maybe you won't. Kill him."

With two headshots, Frankie's body fell into the river. Felipe watched as his body floated upstream.

***

Jamila picked up the phone and called Lorenzo, and he picked up after two rings.

"Hello?"

"Lorenzo, I haven't heard from you since the party. What you been up to?"

"Hey, Jamila, I'm just taking care of a few things and going over the new numbers coming in. Just making sure I don't skip a beat."

"That's good to hear. Well, I have a meeting with a few members from the Temple tomorrow afternoon."

"About what?" asked Lorenzo.

"I don't know, but I wanted you to come with me."

"What time?"

"Three p.m.," replied Jamila.

"Sure, I'll meet up with you around two p.m. tomorrow and we will go together."

"Okay, I'll see you tomorrow then."

"Hey, Jamila, one more thing. The Landon family is doing good business with us now too. And I want you to go over these numbers with me tomorrow."

"Sure, I'll go over the numbers with you after the meeting. I'll see you tomorrow, Lorenzo."

After hanging up the phone, she saw that Carlos was calling.

"Hello, Carlos."

"Hello, Jamila, I was calling to let you know I'm sending someone there to come to talk to you for me. They will be up there this week."

"Okay, I will be waiting on them."

"I'll call you when they are on the way," replied Carlos.

"Thank you, Carlos."

"No problem, Jamila."

SAYNOMORE

Chapter 52

Oso walked to the back of Morwell's house, where Morwell was sitting at the pool looking at the females swim nude as he smoked his cigar, even sniffing his lines of cocaine.

"I'm back, Morwell," said Oso.

Morwell turned around to look at Oso, blowing smoke from his mouth.

"Come have a seat with me, little brother. So, tell me, were the rumors true about Jamila buying from Felipe?"

"Yes, they were."

"So, did you kill her?" asked Morwell.

"No, she had a good reason why she was spending with him."

"So, tell me this good reason, little brother."

"Felipe killed her father twenty years ago and raped her mother. So, she just wanted to get close enough to kill him."

"But he's not dead, Oso, so how you know she ain't just tell you that?" replied Morwell.

"I don't think she would lie to me, considering the respect she has for you, even the loyalty she showed you all these years," replied Oso.

"You do remember Cocha?"

"Yes, I do, Morwell."

"He showed me respect and loyalty for twenty plus years and he chose to tell me to my face he didn't betray me after I asked him more than one time to tell me the truth. So, I showed him he was lying, then I gutted him like a fish. So, my question to you is how you know she's telling the truth?"

"Because she killed Jatavious Stone who was with Felipe when they raped her mother and killed her father."

Morwell took his cigar out of his mouth and said, "That's why nobody can find him. I was wrong to question her loyalty to us. She was just waiting on the right time to strike and she did."

Morwell took another pull of his cigar. "She is a thinker, Oso. She can be fatal to us in the future. So what is she going to do about Felipe?"

"She's trying to figure that out now, but I just got back. So, if we are done I would like to go take a shower."

"Yes, we are done, brother."

Chapter 53

Jamila woke up at 8:30 p.m. that morning. She took a shower and turned her phone on, and that's when a text came in from Carlos that said: *APPLEBEES for lunch on 110th and Lennox.* She replied back: *OK, I'll be there.*

Carlos added: *his name is Martinez and he'll be waiting for you at noon.*

Jamila made it to the restaurant at 11:45 a.m. When she walked in, she saw a Spanish man sitting next to a young lady, and he waved her over.

"Hello, Jamila," the young lady said.

"Hola," the man said.

Jamila looked at the young lady.

"He doesn't speak English, but he said hello to you."

"Tell him I said hello as well."

He said something else in Spanish.

"He said how can he help you?"

"Tell him I have a little problem I need help with. It's Felipe."

The lady turned and told him to speak in Spanish. He looked at Jamila, took his hat off, and wiped his face with a handkerchief. He said something to her again. She looked at Jamila.

The young lady translated the man's words: "He said what type of problem?"

Jamila picked up her glass of water that was at the table, and took a sip and then she started speaking in Spanish to him. His eyes opened wide when Jamila switched over to Spanish.

"Mister, I already spoke to Carlos, so I know you can speak English. So, are we going to handle business or are you going to waste my time?" replied Jamila.

"I see you are good, Jamila. He told me you were. So, tell me, what is the problem?"

"I want Felipe dead yesterday. I can have my own man come down there and do it. I just need your help to help him move around while he is down there. Or, I can just pay up to four hundred thousand dollars to have someone else take care of it for me."

"Jamila, what you are saying is a lot, but I will get in touch with Carlos and let him know what we talked about. I'm telling you now, Jamila, Felipe runs the Dominican Republic. He is untouchable down there, but I do believe that anybody can get killed. A lot of people do want him dead. Nonetheless, I will be in touch with you, Jamila."

"I'll be waiting on your call, Martinez, and you two have a blessed day."

Jamila got up and walked away from the table to her car. When she made it back to Jelani's, she and Lorenzo went to the Temple.

"Jamila, so what is this place?"

"Lorenzo, I don't know, but whoever they are—they are powerful and it might be good for us."

Once they walked inside, they made their way to the office, where they saw people sitting at a table looking at them. One person was standing like he was King Arthur and this was his round table.

"Jamila, Lorenzo, please come have a seat. My name is Trayvon and no disrespect to you, but my name will be the only name that will be told to you at this table."

"I understand, Trayvon. So, please tell me, what can I do for you?"

"Jamila, it just came to us that you are the rightful owner of the Oceanfront Property."

"Yes, I am."

"We need to buy it from you."

"It's not for sale," replied Jamila.

"Let's work out a deal."

"Trayvon, there's no deal to work out, but please let me hear what you have to offer."

"A seat at this table," a voice from the back of the room said.

Jamila looked at Lorenzo, smiled, and shook her head.

"Can you tell me what's the big deal at a seat at this table?"

198

"Because, Jamila, the table you sit at now with us—the other families wish they can have a seat at this table with us. We are offering you a part of history. We all know how you came up to be who you are today, queen don. We have our eyes on you and Lorenzo."

"So, tell me, *sir* in the back, why is my property so important to you and if this table is so great why don't you just take it from me?"

"Because we are true and honest at this table and that would break the bounds at this table we stand on."

"No disrespect to you, but just because a line looks straight doesn't mean it ain't crooked and you never told me why you want my property."

"Because that is the only property that stops us from having the whole borderline. Your father knew what he was doing when he got that property."

"This is what I will do. I will hand over forty-eight percent of the property to the Temple and I ask that you let me and Lorenzo have a seat at this table with ya. Whatever you do with the property is up to you. I don't want to know, it ain't my business, do we have a deal?" asked Jamila.

Jamila watched as he looked around at everyone at the table, and five of them nodded while two of them shook their heads.

"Jamila, you have a deal—Thank you all for your time," said Trayvon.

When Jamila and Lorenzo walked out of the Temple, Lorenzo looked at her.

"Damn! Jamila, you really are a tough cookie. So, what now?"

"I hope Carlos helps me out with this Felipe problem."

"What vibe did you get from the meeting early today with his people?" asked Lorenzo.

"A good vibe."

"So, you know Symone's been doing a good job with *Passions*."

"Yeah, I know, Lorenzo. So, what are these numbers you were talking about yesterday to me?"

"With each of the businesses we are up by forty percent and with the last of the powder we made back six times the original investment and still have much more right now."

"That's good to hear," replied Jamila.

"So, did you tell Frankie we will not be putting our families together?"

"No, I did not, Lorenzo."

"When was the last time you heard from him?" asked Lorenzo.

"The night of the party. I'll pay him a visit sometime this week and I will tell him then."

Jamila dropped Lorenzo off at Jelani's, and went to her condo.

Chapter 54

"Hey, beautiful, come here let me talk to you for a minute."

"What's up, Badii?"

"Nothing, trying to see what you got going on tonight, Tasha."

"Whatever, Badii, you trying to fuck me tonight, that's all."

"There you go, Tasha, it's nothing like that."

"So, that's why you pulled up in the park just to see what I'm getting into tonight?" asked Tasha.

"Yeah, facts. You know—just a little smoke session— just the two of us," replied Badii.

"You got so much game, I swear, you do."

Badii just smiled to himself as Tasha was talking.

"Badii, you clean, right?"

"Yeah, why?"

"Because you have a detective walking this way towards us."

Badii turned around and saw Detective Boatman walking up to him, smoking a *Black & Mild*.

"Yo, Tasha, step off. I'll pull back up on you in a minute."

"You sure?"

"Yeah, I got this."

Tasha went walking off as Detective Boatman walked up.

"It's a nice evening in the park, don't you think?"

"What can I do for you, detective?" asked Badii.

"I was thinking we can help each other out."

"I don't help out your kind. Matter of fact, I don't even talk to your kind."

"And what's my kind?" replied Boatman.

"Pigs in a blanket. So, if you don't mind, part my back."

Detective Boatman looked at Badii's waist and saw the handle to the gun he had on him. He looked around to see who was watching them; he saw he had a few eyes on him.

"Hold on a second, what's that you have on your waist?" said Detective Boatman.

Badii turned around and looked at Detective Boatman.

"Don't even try me, you know what it is."

"I don't know shit."

Detective Boatman walked towards Badii. Seeing him approaching, Badii bit his bottom lip then looked at Tasha as he pulled out to shoot Detective Boatman. Boatman saw the move in his wrist already, and was prepared for it. Before Badii could pull the trigger, Boatman shot him three times in the chest, dropping him. Once Badii hit the ground, he kicked his gun away from him.

"What the fuck you do some dumb shit like that for?"

Detective Boatman pulled out his radio, and called it in as he looked at everyone coming his way.

"Stay back, stay back," he said, pointing his gun into the crowd.

Tasha just looked at Badii lying dead on the ground with his eyes open, looking into space in a pool of his own blood. Masi was walking past the park when he saw all the police standing around in the park. Then he heard Tasha call his name.

"Yoo, what's up, Tasha? What's going on over there?"

"They just killed Badii, they just killed him, Masi."

"Who killed Badii, who?"

"It was Detective Boatman, you know who he is."

Masi ran across the street to where everyone was in the park, just in time to see them covering up Badii's body with a white sheet.

"Fuck, man! Damn. I know they ain't do my nigga like that. Fuck!"

Masi and Detective Boatman caught eye contact. Before walking off in the crowd, Masi pointed two fingers at him and shot at him, letting him know he was a dead man walking. Detective Boatman just looked at him as he walked away.

***

Masi walked into Jelani's straight to Jamila's office. When he walked through the doors, Jamila and Lorenzo were sitting at the table, talking.

"Masi, I'm glad you came in. Have a seat, we need to talk."

"Jamila, before we talk, I got some fucked up news."

Jamila looked at Masi and then Lorenzo.

"And what is this news you have?"

"Detective Boatman just killed Badii in the park, shot him down."

Jamila got up and put her hands on the table.

"What the fuck you telling me this muthafucker just killed Badii? Lorenzo, you and Masi go down there and see what the fuck just happened. If that nigga killed Badii, I want his fucking head on an ice pick."

Jamila watched as they walked out of her office. She pulled Detective Boatman's card out of her desk drawer and texted him: *You know you done fucked up now.*

She walked to the sliding door in her office, and looked out to see Masi and Lorenzo pulling off. She turned around to hear her phone ringing. She walked over to the table and picked it up.

"Hello."

"Hello, Jamila. I hope I ain't catch you at a bad time."

"It's okay, Carlos, I spoke to your associate you had come to see me."

"Yes, they told me they were very impressed with you, but I'm calling you now because I have some bad news to tell you."

"Let me guess, you can't help me with the Felipe problem."

"Jamila, under the new circumstances we are going to help you, but I'm sorry to tell you this—The local authorities down here found a body floating in the river and it was Frankie."

"Oh my God! Don't tell me that, Carlos, are you sure?"

"Yes, he had three bullet holes to the head. I had a female friend of mine go claim his body today. Jamila, he came down here to talk to Felipe about you, he broke the rules."

"Carlos, can I call you back please?" asked Jamila.

"Yes, you can."

Jamila sat down as tears started flowing from her eyes. Frankie was more to her than a friend, he was a father figure too. She picked up the phone and called Lorenzo.

"Hey, Jamila, we are just pulling up now."

"Lorenzo, I just got a call from Carlos, he told me Felipe killed Frankie."

"Are you for real, Jamila?" replied Lorenzo, stunned by the news.

"Yeah, he went to talk to Felipe about me and he killed him."

"What are you going to do now?"

"I hate to say it, but I'm going to see Fabio. I'm about to take a flight out tonight."

"Do you want me to come with you?" asked Lorenzo.

"No, I need you here to take care of this Badii problem and to see what happened with that.

"I'm on it."

Jamila closed her eyes, then went to get ready for her flight.

Chapter 55

Jamila's plane landed in Paris at 10 o'clock that night. She had reservations at the Plaza Inn in Lovate. Jamila couldn't get Frankie out of her mind, and all night she thought about him. From the good times, even the bad times, to all that they had been through. It was 9 o'clock that morning when Jamila got ready to go see Fabio. She had on black three-inch stiletto heels, and a black Louis Vuitton dress that came down to her calf. Her hair was pressed, with curls at the tips. Her dress showed just a little cleavage and it was tight around her waist, showing her shape. She was wearing her three-carat earrings and tennis bracelet when the taxi pulled up at the hotel. Paris was so beautiful, and Fabio had three of the best restaurants you could eat at. When Jamila walked inside, she saw the same layout as Jelani's, but there weren't any cameras and the chandeliers were different colors. Jamila walked right past the front desk to the elevator. When she made it to his office door, she heard him talking to someone. She stood there by the door, and listened.

"So, it's done? He's dead?"

"Yes, Fabio, it was taken care of a few days ago. Felipe told me to tell you he did what you asked him to do. Now you must keep your end of the deal. He wants to know a time frame?"

"Tell him after Frankie's funeral, she'll be dead—And I'll make sure she feels every fucking thing," replied Fabio.

"You know, what I don't understand is why kill him? He loved you. I know you and Felipe are going into business with each other but still—"

"He was in my way. Now that he is dead, his family is my family to run now. And with Jamila dead, Queens and the Bronx will be mine."

"If truth be told, Fabio, Frankie treated you like a son."

"He put that bitch in front of me. I gave her what I had. I made her, I made her. It took me some time to figure it out, but I did. Now I have an endless supply of cocaine."

"So, how you going to say you heard about his death?"

"Jamila is going to tell me, I'm sure about it," said Fabio.

Jamila turned around and walked off back down the hall. She put her sunglasses on and made it to the front door. She turned around when she heard someone say, "Mrs. LaCross." Jamila turned around and saw Tamera holding a little boy. He was sleeping in her arms, and he looked just like Fabio. Jamila looked at Tamera; she was very beautiful. She was at least 5'6 tall with long, honey-blonde hair. She looked to be French. Her eyes were hazelnut, and her skin was a shade darker than yellow. Her son opened his eyes, and looked at Jamila. She took her glasses off and looked into his green eyes. She couldn't help but smile at him. He waved to her, and she waved back before turning and walking away. Jamila made it back to her hotel and caught the next flight out to NYC. Taking out her phone, she called Lorenzo.

"Hey, how is your trip?"

"I'm on my way back now. I should be landing in a few hours. Make sure you be on standby when I land to pick me up from the airport."

"I'll be ready and I'll tell you the story of what happened to Badii when I pick you up," said Lorenzo.

"Okay, I'll talk to you when my plane lands. I'll see you soon."

Jamila put her phone up, knowing she was going to kill Fabio in the worst way.

***

"So, you telling me that Fabio had Frankie killed?"

"Yes, I heard it myself. He was talking to someone in his office when I walked up to the door. I heard every word he said. Now I know how Felipe knew where I lived and how the rope got put in my house."

"So, what now?" asked Lorenzo.

"I'm going to kill Fabio's ass. Let me call him now, hold up."

"Hello."

"Hey, Fabio!"

206

"Hey, Jamila, is everything okay?"

"No, I just got a phone call telling me that Frankie is dead."

"What? Say that again?" replied Fabio.

"Yes, Frankie is dead, Fabio, he's dead. Someone killed him."

"Are you sure?"

"Yeah, I am."

"Where did he get killed at?" asked Fabio.

"Mexico, his body just got up here a few hours ago."

"Okay, I'm coming out there, Jamila. I'll be there tomorrow to see you."

"Okay," replied Jamila.

Fabio hung up the phone, and picked his son up.

"Daddy, daddy!"

"What's up, little man?"

"I saw her."

"Who?" asked Fabio.

"*Her* on your phone."

"You saw her."

"Yes, I waved to her. Daddy, come play the game with me."

"Here I come now, just give me a few minutes."

Fabio looked at his phone and said to himself: "No, he couldn't have seen her, kids—" He laughed to himself as he walked off.

"So, tell me now what happened with Badii."

"From what I was told it was a hit. Detective Boatman walked up to him and killed him. He knew Badii had a gun on him, so he had all rights to do what he did."

Jamila just looked out the window as Lorenzo was driving.

"Have someone give his family one point five million dollars and see if you can find out where Detective Boatman lives. I want him dead after we get whatever he has on our family. So, we don't get fucked over in the end."

"I'll get on it right away.

SAYNOMORE

Chapter 56

It's been six days since Frankie's death, and his funeral was later in the day. Jamila, Symone, Lorenzo, Masi, and a few more members of the LaCross family were there. Each other family was there as well. It was over two hundred people there. The FBI was outside, taking pictures of everyone. Fabio walked in with two pink roses in his hand. As he walked up to Frankie's casket, he bent over and gave him a kiss on each cheek. He put a rose in his top pocket and the other rose in his hand. When he turned around, he saw Jamila sitting down and nodded to her. She nodded back. Once he sat down, Jamila got up to speak about Frankie, and everyone was looking at her.

"Frankie was more than a friend to me. He was someone I could talk to when I needed to vent." Tears rolled down her face as she spoke. "He never turned his back on me. From day one, his loyalty was till his last breath. He had a heart of pure gold. I remember one day we were eating tomatoes in his garden and he asked me, "*Are you scared to die?*" I told him that I was, and he held out his hand for me to grab and said, "*Why be scared to die? If anything, be scared of life because one day death is going to come.*" I miss him so much. The last thing I told him was, *I'll see you later*. I never got the chance to even say goodbye."

The funeral was three hours long. After it was over, everyone walked outside.

"Jamila, are you alright?"

"Yeah, I'm going down to Mexico tomorrow, Fabio, to where they found his body. Do you want to come with me?" asked Jamila.

"Yeah, I do, I would like that!" replied Fabio.

"Okay, I have to go take care of a few things, so I will call you tomorrow."

Fabio watched Jamila walk back to Lorenzo.

"So, what he say?" asked Lorenzo.

"He's going to come with us tomorrow. Symone, tomorrow I have to go on a trip, so me and Lorenzo are going to need you to handle the clubs. I'm leaving Masi and Slim Boogie with you."

"Okay, I can handle it, sis."

"Okay, look, you, Masi, and Slim Boogie go back to the hotel. Me and Lorenzo have to go pay someone a visit and I will see you tonight."

Jamila walked to the car as Lorenzo opened the limo door for her to get in.

"So, where are we headed?" asked Lorenzo.

"To see Detective Boatman."

"Jamila, I have his address, but he's not there. I had Muscle watching the place all night."

"Who lives there with him?" asked Jamila.

"Nobody, but I do know where his brother stays."

"So, let's go pay his brother a visit."

Jamila just sat quietly as they drove to Detective Boatman's brother's house.

"Lorenzo, is that him out front?"

"Yeah, that's him.

Jamila looked around to see who was standing around. There was nobody outside. The street was quiet, and had just a few cars on the block.

"Wait here, I'll be right back."

Opening up the limo door, Jamila got out and walked over to Detective Boatman's brother's house.

"Excuse me, excuse me."

"Hey, beautiful, how you doing today?"

"I'm doing good, let me introduce myself. My name is Jamila LaCross."

Detective Boatman's brother looked at her and took two steps back. Then he looked at the limo and Lorenzo standing outside of it.

"What can I do for you, Mrs. LaCross?"

"To be honest, I was going to come over here and kill you and your family because of your brother's actions, but I'm not. I just want you to tell your brother I stopped by and he knows he fucked up. Can you do that for me?" asked Jamila.

"Yeah, I can do that."

Jamila looked at him, then walked up to him and gave him a kiss on the cheek.

"Thank you, sweetheart!"

She turned around and walked away.

SAYNOMORE

Chapter 57

Fabio called Jamila at nine that morning.

"Hey, Jamila, I have a private plane to take us to Mexico."

"No, Fabio, I have a plane."

"Okay then, I'll come fly with you then. What time we leaving?"

"Be at the airport by eleven a.m. Lorenzo will be out front waiting on you."

"Okay."

Jamila put her phone in her bag, and looked in the mirror. She had a plan, and she needed Fabio to help her pull it off. Lorenzo saw when Fabio pulled up.

"So, you ready, Fabio?"

"Ready for what? To see where Frankie was found at? Yeah, I am. Lorenzo, that man took me in when nobody else would. I loved him and I will kill whoever did this to him."

"That's how Jamila feels also. Come on, let's make it to the plane."

Once they got off the plane in Mexico, Carlos had a car there ready to pick them up.

"So Jamila, where did he get killed at?"

"I don't know, Fabio, I just know where they found his body at?"

"So, where are we going now?" asked Fabio.

"To a friend of Frankie's who claimed the body so he can take us where he was found at."

When they pulled up at Carlos's house, he came to the door to meet them.

"Hello, Jamila, it's good to finally meet you!"

"Likewise. This is Lorenzo, Fabio, and Muscle."

"Please, all of you, follow me inside."

As they walked the door, Jamila couldn't believe how beautiful Carlos's house was.

"Fabio, isn't this house beautiful?" asked Jamila.

"Yes, it is."

At that point two men grabbed Fabio.

"What the fuck you got going on? Get the fuck up off me?"

Jamila just watched as Carlos walked up to him and stuck a needle in his neck.

"Good night, Fabio."

"What the hell!" were his last words before he went to sleep.

"Should we get started, Jamila?" asked Carlos.

"Yes, we should. Let's cut him open and put C-4 in him."

When Fabio woke up, he was tied down and stripped to his boxers. Opening his eyes, everything seemed blurry.

"What the fuck you do to me?"

Jamila picked up a chair, and placed it down in front of him.

"How you feel, sweetheart?" asked Jamila.

"What did you do to me?"

"We did a lot to you, Fabio. And I saw your son a few days ago, he looks just like you. See, I came to talk to you face to face to tell you what happened with Frankie and just before I could knock on your door, I overheard the whole conversation you had on how you set him up to get killed. Even on how you were going to have me killed after Frankie's funeral. I heard everything you had to say. You killed a man who loved you as his son, now look at you."

"You know what, Jamila? Fuck you and Frankie. I don't regret anything I did and I'm ready to take whatever comes my way, bitch."

"I'll show you your bitch," replied Jamila with rage in her eyes.

She got up and walked up to Lorenzo. He handed her a baseball bat. Fabio looked at her right as she swung it and smacked him in the face with it.

"Who the bitch now, pussy? Who?" She hit him in the ribs and legs. Fabio screamed as blood came from his body. Jamila beat him until Lorenzo and Muscle pulled her off of him. Fabio was laying there with blood coming from his face, legs, and a broken arm. Carlos just looked at her.

"Jamila, you ready to drop him off?" asked Carlos.

214

"Yeah, let's get this over with. Where is the book bag at, Lorenzo?"

"Right here, Jamila."

"Good, here ya go as promised, one point five million dollars in cash."

Both guards looked at the money, picked Fabio up, and put him in the trunk. Jamila just looked at them.

"Don't worry, Jamila, they are police officers who just guard Felipe's house, but they work for me. They are going to drop Fabio off at the front of Felipe's house just as agreed to. And trust me, Felipe is going to come out to see what's going on. That's when we will kill two birds with one stone, as you Americans say."

Jamila watched from down the block on the hill as they dropped Fabio's body off at Felipe's gate in the front of his house. She watched Felipe and six of his men come outside to the gates, looking at Fabio.

"What happened to him?"

"We don't know, Felipe, we found him this way."

Felipe turned Fabio over, then he stood him up and looked around. All Fabio said was, "Jamila."

"You two, just drop him off. Go see if you can find her now."

Jamila kept watching. She saw Carlos's two men go back in the car and drove off. Carlos looked at Jamila, and she nodded. That's when Carlos pressed the button, and Fabio's body blew up Felipe and his men. Jamila just stood there and watched for a minute before leaving.

"Jamila, it's done."

"It is, thank you, Carlos!"

"Thank you, Jamila."

When Jamila made it back to New York, she was in her office, looking at the picture of her and Fabio when he took her to Paris. She got up and walked to the fireplace and threw the picture in the fire. *Felipe told Frankie I was good and he was great. I guess he was wrong because even though good is the enemy of greatness, greatness must be in me because still I stand. I did what my father did, but better. I avenged his death. I know he's proud of me. Now I can live knowing that the day I saw him being killed on videotape took me many years, but just know he didn't die alone.*

Chapter 58

The Next Day

Jamila walked into Jelani's.

"Mrs. LaCross, you have a package here, it was dropped off this morning."

Jamila walked over to the desk, and picked up the box.

"Thank you, Jackie!"

As she made her way to her office, she placed the box down on her desk, and took her coat off to hang it up. When she opened the box, it was all the videos and pictures of her when she killed both of Deniro's men. Detective Boatman had been in possession of these videos and pictures until he sent them now with a note that said: *There are no copies.* Jamila smiled to herself, knowing Detective Boatman got her message. She walked to her hidden office, and placed the box in the safe, knowing in her heart that there was still a copy out there, and that he was a dead man walking.

***

Morwell was smoking his cigar, looking at the news when Oso walked up to him.

"I guess you were right, Oso, she did have a reason to get close to him. She killed him and his men."

"Brother, I have to ask you something."

"And what's that, Oso?" asked Morwell.

"I know why you said you killed our other brother because he wasn't loyal to us and was working for the enemy, but what proof did you ever have?"

"Oso, I don't want to talk about this anymore. We talked about this over and over again. I saw him with them, that's all you need to know. Now don't come to me with this again. Papa told me sometimes the greatest pain comes from the ones you love the most."

Morwell put his cigar down, turned around, and saw Oso pointing the .45 in his face.

"So, this is the end of Morwell and the beginning of Oso."

"Damn, brother!"

Bang!

Bang!

To Be Continued . . .
Mob Ties 4
Coming Soon

Submission Guideline

Submit the first three chapters of your completed manuscript to ldpsubmissions@gmail.com, subject line: Your book's title. The manuscript must be in a .doc file and sent as an attachment. Document should be in Times New Roman, double spaced and in size 12 font. Also, provide your synopsis and full contact information. If sending multiple submissions, they must each be in a separate email.

Have a story but no way to send it electronically? You can still submit to LDP/Ca$h Presents. Send in the first three chapters, written or typed, of your completed manuscript to:

LDP: Submissions Dept
Po Box 944
Stockbridge, Ga 30281

DO NOT send original manuscript. Must be a duplicate.

Provide your synopsis and a cover letter containing your full contact information.

Thanks for considering LDP and Ca$h Presents.

<u>NEW RELEASES</u>

FRIEND OR FOE 3 by MIMI
A GANGSTA'S KARMA by FLAME
NIGHTMARE ON SILENT AVE by CHRIS GREEN
THE STREETS MADE ME 3 by LARRY D. WRIGHT
MOBBED UP 3 by KING RIO
JACK BOYZ N DA BRONX 3 by ROMELL TUKES
A DOPE BOY'S QUEEN 3 by ARYANNA
MOB TIES 3 by SAYNOMORE

SAYNOMORE

STREET KINGS III

PAID IN BLOOD III

CARTEL KILLAZ IV

DOPE GODS III

Hood Rich

SINS OF A HUSTLA II

ASAD

RICH $AVAGE II

By Troublesome

YAYO V

Bred In The Game 2

S. Allen

CREAM III

By Yolanda Moore

SON OF A DOPE FIEND III

HEAVEN GOT A GHETTO II

By Renta

LOYALTY AIN'T PROMISED III

By Keith Williams

I'M NOTHING WITHOUT HIS LOVE II

SINS OF A THUG II

TO THE THUG I LOVED BEFORE II

By Monet Dragun

QUIET MONEY IV

EXTENDED CLIP III

THUG LIFE IV

By **Trai'Quan**

THE STREETS MADE ME IV

By **Larry D. Wright**

IF YOU CROSS ME ONCE II

By **Anthony Fields**
THE STREETS WILL NEVER CLOSE II
By **K'ajji**
HARD AND RUTHLESS III
Von Diesel
KILLA KOUNTY II
By **Khufu**
MOBBED UP IV
By **King Rio**
MONEY GAME II
By **Smoove Dolla**
A GANGSTA'S KARMA II
By **FLAME**
JACK BOYZ VERSUS DOPE BOYZ
By **Romell Tukes**
MOB TIES IV
By **SayNoMore**

Available Now

RESTRAINING ORDER **I & II**
By **CA$H & Coffee**
LOVE KNOWS NO BOUNDARIES **I II & III**
By **Coffee**
RAISED AS A GOON I, II, III & IV
BRED BY THE SLUMS I, II, III
BLAST FOR ME I & II
ROTTEN TO THE CORE I II III
A BRONX TALE I, II, III

SAYNOMORE

DUFFLE BAG CARTEL I II III IV V VI

HEARTLESS GOON I II III IV V

A SAVAGE DOPEBOY I II

DRUG LORDS I II III

CUTTHROAT MAFIA I II

KING OF THE TRENCHES

By **Ghost**

LAY IT DOWN **I & II**

LAST OF A DYING BREED I II

BLOOD STAINS OF A SHOTTA I & II III

By **Jamaica**

LOYAL TO THE GAME I II III

LIFE OF SIN I, II III

By **TJ & Jelissa**

BLOODY COMMAS I & II

SKI MASK CARTEL I II & III

KING OF NEW YORK I II,III IV V

RISE TO POWER I II III

COKE KINGS I II III IV

BORN HEARTLESS I II III IV

KING OF THE TRAP I II

By **T.J. Edwards**

IF LOVING HIM IS WRONG…I & II

LOVE ME EVEN WHEN IT HURTS I II III

By **Jelissa**

WHEN THE STREETS CLAP BACK I & II III

THE HEART OF A SAVAGE I II III

By **Jibril Williams**

A DISTINGUISHED THUG STOLE MY HEART I II & III

LOVE SHOULDN'T HURT I II III IV

RENEGADE BOYS I II III IV
PAID IN KARMA I II III
SAVAGE STORMS I II
AN UNFORESEEN LOVE
By **Meesha**
A GANGSTER'S CODE I &, II III
A GANGSTER'S SYN I II III
THE SAVAGE LIFE I II III
CHAINED TO THE STREETS I II III
BLOOD ON THE MONEY I II III
By J-Blunt
PUSH IT TO THE LIMIT
By **Bre' Hayes**
BLOOD OF A BOSS **I, II, III, IV, V**
SHADOWS OF THE GAME
TRAP BASTARD
By **Askari**
THE STREETS BLEED MURDER **I, II & III**
THE HEART OF A GANGSTA I II& III
By **Jerry Jackson**
CUM FOR ME I II III IV V VI VII
An **LDP Erotica Collaboration**
BRIDE OF A HUSTLA **I II & II**
THE FETTI GIRLS **I, II& III**
CORRUPTED BY A GANGSTA I, II III, IV
BLINDED BY HIS LOVE
THE PRICE YOU PAY FOR LOVE I, II ,III
DOPE GIRL MAGIC I II III
By **Destiny Skai**
WHEN A GOOD GIRL GOES BAD

SAYNOMORE

By **Adrienne**
THE COST OF LOYALTY I II III
By Kweli
A GANGSTER'S REVENGE **I II III & IV**
THE BOSS MAN'S DAUGHTERS I II III IV V
A SAVAGE LOVE **I & II**
BAE BELONGS TO ME I II
A HUSTLER'S DECEIT I, II, III
WHAT BAD BITCHES DO I, II, III
SOUL OF A MONSTER I II III
KILL ZONE
A DOPE BOY'S QUEEN I II III
By **Aryanna**
A KINGPIN'S AMBITON
A KINGPIN'S AMBITION **II**
I MURDER FOR THE DOUGH
By **Ambitious**
TRUE SAVAGE I II III IV V VI VII
DOPE BOY MAGIC I, II, III
MIDNIGHT CARTEL I II III
CITY OF KINGZ I II
NIGHTMARE ON SILENT AVE
By **Chris Green**
A DOPEBOY'S PRAYER
By **Eddie "Wolf" Lee**
THE KING CARTEL **I, II & III**
By **Frank Gresham**
THESE NIGGAS AIN'T LOYAL **I, II & III**
By **Nikki Tee**
GANGSTA SHYT **I II &III**

By **CATO**
THE ULTIMATE BETRAYAL
By **Phoenix**
BOSS'N UP **I , II & III**
By **Royal Nicole**
I LOVE YOU TO DEATH
By **Destiny J**
I RIDE FOR MY HITTA
I STILL RIDE FOR MY HITTA
By **Misty Holt**
LOVE & CHASIN' PAPER
By **Qay Crockett**
TO DIE IN VAIN
SINS OF A HUSTLA
By **ASAD**
BROOKLYN HUSTLAZ
By **Boogsy Morina**
BROOKLYN ON LOCK I & II
By **Sonovia**
GANGSTA CITY
By **Teddy Duke**
A DRUG KING AND HIS DIAMOND I & II III
A DOPEMAN'S RICHES
HER MAN, MINE'S TOO I, II
CASH MONEY HO'S
THE WIFEY I USED TO BE I II
By Nicole Goosby
TRAPHOUSE KING **I II & III**
KINGPIN KILLAZ I II III
STREET KINGS I II

PAID IN BLOOD **I II**
CARTEL KILLAZ I II III
DOPE GODS I II
By **Hood Rich**
LIPSTICK KILLAH **I, II, III**
CRIME OF PASSION I II & III
FRIEND OR FOE I II III
By **Mimi**
STEADY MOBBN' **I, II, III**
THE STREETS STAINED MY SOUL I II
By **Marcellus Allen**
WHO SHOT YA **I, II, III**
SON OF A DOPE FIEND I II
HEAVEN GOT A GHETTO
Renta
GORILLAZ IN THE BAY **I II III IV**
TEARS OF A GANGSTA I II
3X KRAZY I II
DE'KARI
TRIGGADALE I II III
Elijah R. Freeman
GOD BLESS THE TRAPPERS I, II, III
THESE SCANDALOUS STREETS I, II, III
FEAR MY GANGSTA I, II, III IV, V
THESE STREETS DON'T LOVE NOBODY I, II
BURY ME A G I, II, III, IV, V
A GANGSTA'S EMPIRE I, II, III, IV
THE DOPEMAN'S BODYGAURD I II
THE REALEST KILLAZ I II III
THE LAST OF THE OGS I II III

Tranay Adams
THE STREETS ARE CALLING
Duquie Wilson
MARRIED TO A BOSS I II III
By Destiny Skai & Chris Green
KINGZ OF THE GAME I II III IV V
Playa Ray
SLAUGHTER GANG I II III
RUTHLESS HEART I II III
By Willie Slaughter
FUK SHYT
By Blakk Diamond
DON'T F#CK WITH MY HEART I II
By Linnea
ADDICTED TO THE DRAMA I II III
IN THE ARM OF HIS BOSS II
By Jamila
YAYO I II III IV
A SHOOTER'S AMBITION I II
BRED IN THE GAME
By S. Allen
TRAP GOD I II III
RICH $AVAGE
By Troublesome
FOREVER GANGSTA
GLOCKS ON SATIN SHEETS I II
By Adrian Dulan
TOE TAGZ I II III
LEVELS TO THIS SHYT I II
By Ah'Million

SAYNOMORE

KINGPIN DREAMS I II III
By Paper Boi Rari
CONFESSIONS OF A GANGSTA I II III
By Nicholas Lock
I'M NOTHING WITHOUT HIS LOVE
SINS OF A THUG
TO THE THUG I LOVED BEFORE
By Monet Dragun
CAUGHT UP IN THE LIFE I II III
By Robert Baptiste
NEW TO THE GAME I II III
MONEY, MURDER & MEMORIES I II III
By **Malik D. Rice**
LIFE OF A SAVAGE I II III
A GANGSTA'S QUR'AN I II III
MURDA SEASON I II III
GANGLAND CARTEL I II III
CHI'RAQ GANGSTAS I II III
KILLERS ON ELM STREET I II III
JACK BOYZ N DA BRONX I II III
A DOPEBOY'S DREAM
By **Romell Tukes**
LOYALTY AIN'T PROMISED I II
By Keith Williams
QUIET MONEY I II III
THUG LIFE I II III
EXTENDED CLIP I II
By **Trai'Quan**
THE STREETS MADE ME I II III
By **Larry D. Wright**

230

THE ULTIMATE SACRIFICE I, II, III, IV, V, VI
KHADIFI
IF YOU CROSS ME ONCE
ANGEL I II
IN THE BLINK OF AN EYE
By **Anthony Fields**
THE LIFE OF A HOOD STAR
By Ca$h & Rashia Wilson
THE STREETS WILL NEVER CLOSE
By K'ajji
CREAM I II
By Yolanda Moore
NIGHTMARES OF A HUSTLA I II III
By King Dream
CONCRETE KILLA I II
By Kingpen
HARD AND RUTHLESS I II
MOB TOWN 251
By Von Diesel
GHOST MOB
Stilloan Robinson
MOB TIES I II III
By SayNoMore
BODYMORE MURDERLAND I II III
By Delmont Player
FOR THE LOVE OF A BOSS
By C. D. Blue
MOBBED UP I II III
By King Rio
KILLA KOUNTY

SAYNOMORE

By Khufu
MONEY GAME
By Smoove Dolla
A GANGSTA'S KARMA
By FLAME

BOOKS BY LDP'S CEO, CA$H

TRUST IN NO MAN

TRUST IN NO MAN 2

TRUST IN NO MAN 3

BONDED BY BLOOD

SHORTY GOT A THUG

THUGS CRY

THUGS CRY 2

THUGS CRY 3

TRUST NO BITCH

TRUST NO BITCH 2

TRUST NO BITCH 3

TIL MY CASKET DROPS

RESTRAINING ORDER

RESTRAINING ORDER 2

IN LOVE WITH A CONVICT

LIFE OF A HOOD STAR

SAYNOMORE